Augusta Joyce Crocheron

Wild Flowers of Deseret

A collection of efforts in verse

Augusta Joyce Crocheron

Wild Flowers of Deseret
A collection of efforts in verse

ISBN/EAN: 9783337105624

Printed in Europe, USA, Canada, Australia, Japan

Cover: Foto ©Andreas Hilbeck / pixelio.de

More available books at **www.hansebooks.com**

WILD FLOWERS

OF

DESERET.

A Collection of Efforts in Verse.

By Augusta Joyce Crocheron.

And I said, "What shall I sing?
  For among those who hear
There will be strangers, friends a few,
  And critics, too, anear."
And one answered, "Listen well,
  And there will come to thee
Out of the silence, faint and low,
  Answering melody."

PRINTED AT THE JUVENILE INSTRUCTOR OFFICE.
Salt Lake City. Utah.
1881.

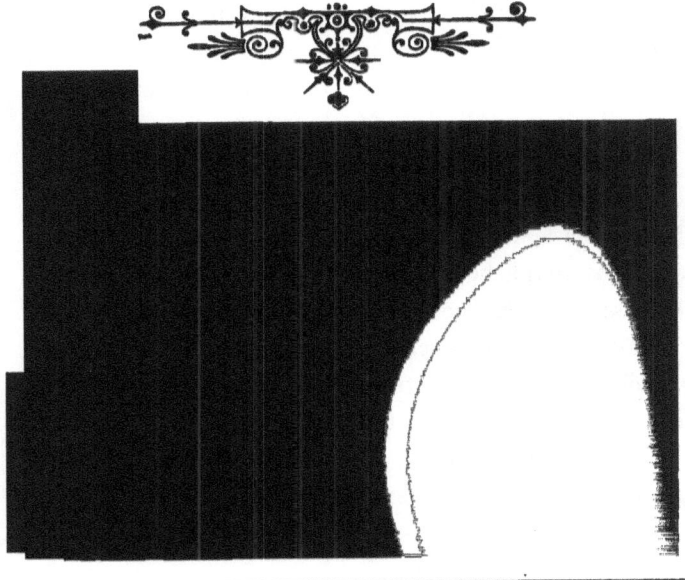

PREFACE.

THE contents of this Volume have been selected from a collection covering a period of twenty years.

. Over a *nome de plume*, a few were published in California, and a few others in St. George, Southern Utah; but to the *Woman's Exponent* I owe my introduction to the literary public.

The idea of publishing in book form had been a thought of the far future; but, upon the advice, and with the kind encouragement of generous friends, this end has been sooner accomplished; and I would here thank those who have so kindly assisted me in its publication.

This volume is presented not so much for its literary excellence: as a memento to those friends who will value the book for the sake of the author.

With this explanation, I hope the reader with whom I am unacquainted will overlook its deficiencies.

A. J. C.

DEDICATION.

To EMMELINE B. WELLS,

　　Editor of *Woman's Exponent,*

　　　　But for whose untiring encouragement
and friendship my efforts would have remained in the
obscurity of my desk, this volume is dedicated, wishing it
were a more worthy tribute, and that it may prove an
acceptable surprise.

　　　　With sincere gratitude and love,

　　　　　　AUGUSTA JOYCE CROCHERON.

CONTENTS.

VIII. CONTENTS.

INTRODUCTORY.

WILD FLOWERS OF DESERET.

GUARDING the hidden desert land,
The Rocky Mountains nobly stand,
Unchangeable and grand, to-day,
As when the Pioneers found way
Adown the canyon's pathway rude,
Into the valley's solitude.

Dusty and gray, and parched and dry,
Beneath the heat of that July,
Only the sage's ashen green,
And cactus here and there between,
And tiny cups of segoes blue,
Greeted the weary traveler's view.

Where now a hundred streamlets run,
With emerald borders, then were none.
Adown the canyon's rocky bed
The crystal waters foaming sped,
Pouring into the Jordan's tide,
The boon—to thirsty earth denied.

Now, through a city's streets it flows:
"The desert blossoms as the rose,"
And garden homes reach far and wide—
The tourist's wonder and our pride;
And groups of happy children play
Where first we traced our lonely way.

No ancient ruin, grand and gray,
To mark a nation passed away;
But a new Kingdom's life begun,
On freedom's soil 'neath a warm sun
And smiling sky, that yet will be
The fairest home of liberty.

The world may wonder and may wait
To watch its growth, its fruit, its fate.
Sown in the sand, watered by tears,
Sheltered by prayers, guarded by fears,
The world has watched its leaves unfold,
And now its bud and bloom behold.

———

Dear reader, here is offered you,
By one scarce known, a volume new.
No place pretentious does it claim,
But lowly, like its chosen name.

We oft, among the many, find
Those who best love the native kind,
And turn from garden lawns, to roam
Through woods and bring wild flowers home.

And some perhaps to us are sweet,
Because they to our hearts repeat
The story of some happy day,
In childhood spent, far, far away.

And some a brier, too, may bear,
And yet be fragrant and be fair.
For truths, like berries, oft are borne
On vines that show full many a thorn.

E'en the sweet brier's modest grace
Anear the castle wall has place,
Nor prized the less because the poor
Train its sweet branches by the door.

And oftener than some rarer flower,
Love sends unto his lady's bower
The sweet and lowly violet,
To love and poets dearest yet.

And from the many flowers that spring
In Deseret, I cull and bring
A few, dear friends, that I have sought,
Wandering in the fields of thought.

Though many lovelier abound,
Than these my eager heart has found;
Still, when in time to come, we see
Books of rare thought, perchance there'll be
A place within thy fond thought yet
For the "Wild Flowers of Deseret."

MY HARP.

This harp Thou gavest to mine hand—
Tune Thou its strings, that I may bring
In offering to Thee, strains that shall
Be worthy Thine acceptance.   Let
Some echo from that higher life
Give me the key, that I may bring
Forth from its trembling strings that thrill
With every passing wind, full tones,
Bearing no discord to the ear.
Teach me to sing, in purity,
Thy truths, Thy love.   And if, perchance,
Thy wandering minstrel by the song
Shall cause some stranger heart to turn,
And learn its secret, and its source,
And follow Thee; then shall this heart
Have won a blest reward!

ASPIRATION.

From memory's tear-blotted leaf,
  Fade every dream, the bright, the dear!
Fade, memory of every grief,
  And every hope that cost a tear!
I look back on you, calm, to-night,
  My fallen idols, without pain;
My present is so glad and bright,
  Ye cannot shade my heart again.

O night! with closed star-eyes, weep on!
  These gladsome lights shine warmly down.
Truth whispered, "here thy rest is won;"
  What care I for your chill and frown?
My baby smiles up in my face,
  A fair child sings beside my knee,
The room seems lit with heavenly grace;
  These are thy gifts, O Life! to me.

Deep in the dream-world of my youth,
  With purpose true, for many a year,
From out the treasuries of truth,
  Feebly I strove alone to rear
Some structure fair, of usefulness,
  To prove my spirit's work within;
My songs sank into silentness,
  My pictures faded 'neath my pen.

As blossoms, from the cool woods brought,
  Droop in the heart-flushed palms that hold,
My poor expression marred the thought,
  In mystic music to me told.
O power! that woke and stirred my mind
  To work beyond my feeble skill,
I know that yet these hands will wind
  These tangled skeins unto their will.

Yet shall I speak in utterance clear,
  The new things whispered to my heart,
Forgetful, in that time, of fear,
  When I in Thy work bear my part.
O, hearts, lone and misunderstood!
  Enough for us, He knows us best;
Falter not in the purpose good,
  And, when at last from earth we rest,

These lights, that dimly burned, will shine
  With their true splendor. And the eyes
Familiar, that had not divined
  Thy proper self, will recognize ;
And each one in his place and name,
  Shrinking no more in earth-wrought thrall,
Stand understood and unashamed,   ·
  In soul-white beauty before all.

MEMORY AND HOPE.

O MEMORY, sweet Memory!
Come thou and sit beside me here.
  Is there no scene, or face, or tale,
  Your faithful pages can unveil,
Wherein, as in a mirror clear,
  I see my past, sweet Memory?

  Hast thou forgot thine early home,
Within the crescent Golden Gate?
  The gothic cottage, the oak trees,
  With beards of moss swung to the breeze?
The heath where sunset lingered late,
  And o'er the white doves floated home?

  Hast thou forgot that garden rare,
With drooping lilacs, clinging vines?
  The marble vases, latticed seat,
  The mirror-pond, the fern leaves sweet?
The spell, while twilight stars did shine
  O'er shades that wrapt its beauty rare?

Hast thou forgot those pictured halls,
The rooms where music trembled low?
   And noble men and women fair,
   Whose presence, beauty lending there,
Made life like dream-life, while came slow
   The steps of night within those halls?

   Hast thou forgot how ocean's hymn
Uprose while sounds of daylight died; ·
   Calling ye round thy mother's chair,
   Where ye, two sisters, knelt in prayer,
Seeing last, her face thy couch beside,
   And last in dreaming ears, her hymn?

   O Memory! sweet Memory!
How sad the vision thou hast stirred!
   No more on earth her face I see,
   Nor sister fair, who knelt with me
Where heaven was taught in every word;
   Nay, read no more, sweet Memory.

   Once, in the home of shadows thronged,
Since our loved parents passed away,
   We, turning treasured pages o'er,
   Together tried to sing once more
The music of departed days;
   But faltering voices checked the song.

   O! thou, dear friend, sweet Memory,
What He witholds, let us resign.
   Come thou, dear Hope, whose gentle speech,
   The Father's love and wisdom teach,
Illume with calm this heart of mine,
   To weep no more with Memory.

PROFESSOR MORSE.

Art's, wealth's and labor's structures fair,
 Fall wasted where war's heroes walk;
Anguish thrills all the sun-bright air,
 While phantom influences stalk,
Adding fresh terrors even there.

Not wrought of ruin, death and tears,
 Thy triumph's greater than a king's;
Thine shall not fade with coming years,
 Nor home hearts bleed, while answering rings
Back to thy greeting the world's cheers.

An unknown height in knowledge found,
 The world advanced and better made,
Thou sittest, and the world is bound
 By cords thy hands thereon have laid;
And 'neath thy touch the thrill goes round.

Thou speakest,* and the whole wide world
 In reverent attention bends
Towards where freedom's flag's unfurled;
 And from its heart to thee extends
Fame's crown, with love and prayers impearled.

*——In June, 1871, an ovation was tendered Professor S. F. B. Morse, at the Academy of Music, in New York. The wires were united, connecting the civilized world in one line, as it were, and from all these countries, congratulations and expressions of heartfelt good-will were sent to him. At the conclusion he replied as follows:

    Academy of Music, New York,
      June 10, 1871.

Greeting.
 To all the telegraphers throughout the world: "*Peace on earth and good will to man!*" *God bless you all!*
       S. F. B. Morse.
 Thus ended this reception, original and unique in character, differing from any demonstration ever before recorded.

MY HEART AND I.

WE'RE sometimes sad, my heart and I,
  (My heart and I are old-time friends)
And oft when clouds obscure our sky,
  Each unto each confidence lends;
And if by chance you happen near,
Some strange confessions you might hear.

My heart and I are special friends;
  We know each other's weakness, too;
Yet for each other make amends
  For any fault, as friends should do.
My heart, I know, with best intent,
Has wrought me ills it never meant.

Yet I forgive my heart, for I
  Ne'er found a friend that so loved me;
O'er all my faults it doth but sigh,
  Where Reason would reproachful be—
Where even hope would shake her head,
Viewing the future path with dread.

Yet no one but my heart and I
  Know what endeavors we have made
To build our castles fair and high,
  On best foundations ever laid;
And no one but my heart and I
Know how complete a wreck they lie.

We don't repine, my heart and I—
  Failures but teach us how we fell;
And if the grapes are hung too high,
  Some other fruit will do as well:
We, thankful, glean the golden wheat
And sweet strawberries at our feet.

We once made note, my heart and I,
   Perhaps with pardonable pride,
Of youth-time's charms that pleased the eye,
   Where now their phantoms only glide
And solace find; for we are told,
In heaven we'll never more grow old.

In reverie, my heart and I,
   Missing the voice we turned to hear,
Have stood beneath the still night sky,
   Feeling the influence hov'ring near
So blest, that ling'ringly we turned
Homeward, where cheerful hearth-lights burned.

Oft have we felt, my heart and I,
   By lonely bed of pain and fear,
The blessed presence drawing nigh,
   Bidding our drooping spirits cheer.
Behold what faith in God can give,
When e'en the dying turn and live.

Not even thou, best friend, mayest share
   The silent vigils that we keep.
Even the darlings of my prayer
   Loosen their clasping in their sleep.
None hear, while solemn hours go by,
The tidings to my heart and I.

Alone, while loved ones gather round,
   To fill life's mission to the last;
Alone, when judgment all have found,
   Waiting to hear our sentence passed;
Before the changeless Judge on high,
We two shall stand—my heart and I.

Companion-pilgrims evermore,
　　Seeking eternal life to gain,
This solemn vow we make, therefore:
　　Faithful in duty to remain,
True to the Father, throned on high,
And to ourselves—my heart and I.

STRENGTH.

WHAT is true strength? 'Tis to crush back
To the heart's depth the answering word,
Scathing and bitter, and pass on
With quiet face, and tearless eye,
And kindly tone, still mindful of
A child's small woe, nor leave undone
The weary, daily, useful task.
To stand alone, and bury deep
The wrong done by a false friend's lip,
Nor show the world the broken trust,
Nor point the hand that dealt the blow.
With acking brain and wounded feet,
To keep the path, with thorns o'ergrown,
While twilight falls o'er the forest way,
And the friendly hand has left thine own,
That might have led to the open plain.
To keep the path, and to win back all
To the worn, tried heart, who had doubted deep.

A MOTHER.

WHAT words of mine can comfort thee?
For sorrow like thine, none can lift
From off thy heart, or even share.
Yet I too know what thou hast lost,
For I have looked upon her face,
And heard the music of her voice.
Time had been kind to her, and placed
His hand with reverence on her head;
Stole not the light within her eyes,
Laid not his silver on her hair,
Nor robbed her cheek of its fair bloom.

I know, when summer comes, thou'lt plant
The white rose on her sheltered grave;
And violets amid the turf,
And twining vines above her head,
Shall break the sense of loneliness.
But when the winter nights are dark,
When all the lights of heaven are out,
And all the sky is thick with clouds
Hung up on lightning's threads of flame,
And the storm sobs upon the air
Like spirits seeking one they've lost,
Or wailing for one lost in sin;
My own heart hears the cry of thine,
Waking the gloomy hour.

Stars to each moment of the night!
Day hath but one, yet more than these.
So to each moment of our lives
God giveth joy; the life-day sun—
A mother's love. He gives it once
To mortal life. Thy sun has set.
Pray, rest, sleep; and in
The new-life morn, thy sun shall rise
And greet thy soul from death.

A PRAYER.

BECAUSE, that when in death I lie,
With lips mute sealed, all powerless
To bless Thy name, or bend the knee
In gratitude for Thy great love,
My lips would plead for length of life.
But yet I know Thy will is best,
And, Father, give to Thee my life.
O make it whatsoe'er Thou wilt—
A flower blooming in the sun,
Or leafless branch 'neath wintry skies!
And only this, my heart shall ask—
For strength sufficient to endure,
To be named worthy at the end,
The robe, eternal life, to wear.

OLD SONGS.

O, HOW a simple song can waken
    Forgotten, old-time scenes,
That come with pathos, nearly breaking
    The heart that on them leaned!
Old songs! old songs! I cannot hear them,
    But, stealing to my heart,
Come memories once breathing them,
    That will not thence depart.

Old songs! lie silent in the bygones,
    Ye only waken pain
For joys now past beyond recalling,
    Or woes that live again.

O, faded hope! once bright and shining,
    Upborne by wings of prayer;
O, faded love! with hope entwining,   .
    Pure as the sunlit air;
Ye waken from your long, long sleeping,
    At the sweet singer's call,
And worldly eyes again are weeping,
    Beneath the music-thrall.

SUNSET.

How far away the sunset seemed!
Far off along the western hills
The dying day sank faintly down;
Her golden light, spun out in threads,
In chains hung 'round the mountain's brow,
And purpled all the pulsing tide.
And crimson glowed the billowy slopes,
And white the sands lay on the plain;
Then sweetly, purely still, all stayed,
As though fair Nature paused in breath,
Rapt with the picture she had drawn;
As though by silence, holy, still,
The splendid glory might be held.
But came the breath of eve, sweet, faint,
And though with steps light as a child's,
That fears to wake its mother's dream,
It broke the holy stillness there.
Then trooped the living colors back
To heaven, from whence their flight had strayed;
Then faded all the glory out
From sky and sea, from hill and vale,
And in the heavens clear and pale,
The evening star looked calmly down,
As though the earth were pure as she.

A LAGOON.

Down in the gloom, at the mountain base,
Where the scene is lone, and the air is chill,
There's a dark lagoon.*   Its stagnant wave
Is shadowed to blackness by noisome reeds,
That stand like spectres, and grimly bend
As the wind goes by with a whisper wierd.
The black snake glides on the mire below,
The minnows dart to the tangled roots,
And the snail lies still in a tuft of moss.
No tender flower here lifts its head,
With sunny face and odor sweet;
No skylark trills on the air her song;
No tiny nests in the branches hang;
No rays of sunlight, warm and bright,
Gleam on the wave, or silver the dew;
But the wind goes by with hurried breath,
The bittern screams, and the echoes run
In a broken trill, through the skeleton reeds.

A splash! and the wild fowl dives from sight;
The owl in the bordering forest calls;
The raven darkens the air and replies,
And even the water's sullen moan,
And dark chill depth, and terrible hush,
Steal over the heart with sick'ning power.

The narrow trail, like a serpent bends,
Leaving the sunless, slimy banks;
Winding down through a canyon dark,
Out to the warm and sunny plain.

*——Mojave River, California.

FLOWERS OF SPRING.

DAINTY white blossoms, so snowily, airily,
Nodding your white heads above as I pass,
Down from your rocking boughs fluttering, fairily,
Your wee flower-mantles of white to the grass.

And, in the soft gloom of the twilight, ye seem
Wee white wings, warm-folded o'er sprites, here adream
On the brown earth, too rude in its touch, for their bed,
With the moon for a lamp, and a weed at the head.

O! purer than dewdrops, and fairer than moon-rays!
My heart knoweth not which it loveth the best,
Gems of the meadow, of bough, or of vine-sprays,
But claspeth ye all in a tender caress.

Sweet memories rise of the days that are fled—
Bird-music, wave-murmurs, and bees overhead
So drowsily droning, my eyelids down fall
Over dreams, waked again by the oriole's call.

Flowers of the plain, where the warm summer's sun shines,
That whirl with the breezes and smile to the noon;
Flowers that cling to the rocks 'neath the shelt'ring pines,
White nuns weaving prayers to the waterfall's tune.

This wild, unprofaned by man's vain, feeble art,
From the world's toil and jar, like God's day, set apart,
Sheds a calm o'er the heart like the peace of God's love,
And leadeth the soul to His altar above.

O! plenteous jewels! God's handiwork showing,
   Decking brow of the mountain and breast of the plain,
So varied in beauty, such rapture bestowing,
   Earth's greatest of artists vie with Him in vain.

Ah, would I forever might keep in my heart
   The lesson each flower's brief life doth impart;
In beauty fulfilling existence, and bear
   In the heart a sweet incense that others share.

THROUGH THE STORM.

"O, WINTER, wilt thou never go?"
My heart kept sighing sad and low.
I thought of that home far away,
Where loved ones waited, day by day,
For tidings that my willing feet
Were coming, coming, true and fleet.

Yet ever, while mine eager eyes,
Appealing, searched the heavenly skies,
Fell down the softly whispering snow,
So fair, yet sternly answering "no!"
No gleam of blue shone overhead,
But falling flakes and sky of lead.

While still the spring days came and went,
And I imprisoned, ill-content,
Beside my casement watched the snow,
Heart-hungry, sighing still to go,
Gleaming no hope from out the skies,
A lark's song, sweet and clear, did rise !

No plaintive note, but glad and high,
As e'er in sunshine filled the sky.
I could not see the bonny bird,
But still the promise sweet I heard
(Though yet the flakes fell thick and fast),
"Winter is broken, o'er at last."

Since then, though trials 'round me close,
My heart the sweet remembrance holds.
Though I the end may not discern,
My soul in trust to Him doth turn
Who token sent, my heart to warm,
Of light and joy above the storm.

RUTHIE'S CHILD.

And 'twas Ruthie's little child
That the new wife led to-day!
Something in the red lips' smile,
Something in the red-gold curls,
Perfect face and dreamy eyes,
And the dainty, dainty way,

Woke a misty memory,
Pain-enfolded, in my brain.
Something near, yet hid from me,
Something dear, yet lost and far,
Where, and whose, were eyes like these,
That these recalled to me again?

As they passed again I turned,
That sweet face once more to see.
Something in the check that burned,
Something in the tender voice,
Almost shaped the undefined—
Passed, and it had fled from me.

So I, musing, went my way,
Down in tangling dreams more deep.
Something through the busy day,
Something all the lonely eve,
Seemed to sob to my own heart,
And burning eyes to wake my sleep.

Ruthie's baby! Does she know,
That her mother's golden head
Lies cold, where sun rays cannot go,
Where caresses cannot reach,
Blind to her baby's beauty sweet,
Deaf to her baby's music speech?

Blest heaven, no! Adown life's way
Her wee feet go, unconscious all;
No memory-pang to cloud her day,
Nor knows of loving eyes that lean
O'er heaven's hight to follow her,
Lest shadows round her way should fall.

Ruthie's baby, sweet, good by!
I kiss you for your red lips' smile,
So like, her, blended smile and sigh.
From far off scenes that hushed to sleep
My past, I came, and face to face,
Met, loved, lost, Ruthie's little child.

THE LADY AND THE SONG.

WHERE, under the branches, the moonlight fell through,
In the silence and cool of the night, all alone,
Like a vision of sorrow she passed to my view,
And I, pitying, listened the mourner's sad tone.

"Come hither, my darling, the night cometh on,
Thy playmates and pets, to their slumbers have gone.
Ah, where, in the shadows, my love, dost thou stray?
From the heart of thy mother no longer delay.
I'll sing thee the song that thou lovest the best,
And safe in my loving arms rock thee to rest."

So sang the lady, so softly and low,
It was more like a sigh and a prayer than a song,
Out on its cadence her heart seemed to go,
And her sad eyes to follow the star-way along.

And ever, the tender, sweet air that she sung,
When she rocked her fair babe to its sleep on her arm,
Like far away dream-music, fell from her tongue,
As she wandered enwrapped in its memory-charm.

Still fairer the face of the sad mother grew,
Fainter, sweeter, her voice, as she sang sad and low.
We knew she was passing away from our view,
And the heart of the mother was waiting to go.

"I dream night and day, of the great mystery
Of the power that has taken my darling from me.
O, when shall I see her, O, when shall I fold
My babe to my bosom again as of old?
Where art thou, my darling, thy voice did I hear?
O speak once again, for I know thou art near!"

There were tears, tears of joy, for the mother at last,
  Was answered the plea of her fond broken heart.
The losing, the waiting, the myst'ry were past,
  And the mother no more from her loved one shall part.

BED TIME.

WHY should I haste, my baby sweet,
  To lay thee in thy pretty bed?
I miss the patter of thy feet
  Already, and the night has shed
    'Round me a sense of solitude.

Why, weary mothers, do we haste
  To lay our sleeping darlings down?
Is life so hurried, that 'tis waste
  Of time to watch while sleep throws 'round
    Her spell, and holds one picture still?

This little face so sweet, so white,
  These eyes so closed as though they kept
Some mighty secret from our sight,
  Until themselves shall wake to tell
    The new things in the dreamland learned!

What fairer pictures can we find,
  To wake our holiest, deepest thought?
By thy pure light, O child of mine!
  Mine own heart's errors I have sought,
    Striving to near thy purity.

Worth more than learned arguments
    Of teachers groping some lost way,
Or evenings in vain pleasures spent,
        This hour of peace, wherein we may
            Renew the spirit's faith and strength!

I know, when, in sleep's deep repose,
    All self-restraint is thrown away;
The wearied features all disclose
    The struggles of the busy day,
        And oft the soul's unrest they wear.

Could we with childhood's faith complete,
    Lay all the world aside at night,
Leaning, in communings sweet,
    Upon our Father's love, how bright
    . The wakening to the new day!

INVOCATION.

AMID these tangled ways of life,
    So thickly strewn with duty's calls,
Lord, let me not lose, in the strife,
    To fulfil each, 'gainst varied thralls
That rise, remembrance of Thy word to me,
    Remembrance of Thy promises
To they who keep their trust in Thee!
    Nature is Thine, calm, clear and pure!
These walls we pass our lives within—
    No wonder brief and insecure
Our resolutions over sins
    That tempt us beyond governing—

Imprisoned in their dull routine
    Of dull, same duties, each and all,
The soul longs for a rest between,
    Unbroken by their harsh recall
Back to the time the heart knew not
    A jar upon its upward dream—
Its pure imaginings of what
    The source, from whence life's mystic stream.
O Thou far Friend! forget not me,
    Though wandering in my lone, lost way
On earth, oft times I have missed Thee.
    Call me; my heart shall hear; the word
Shall lead me to Thyself once more;
    And, rising like the loosened bird,
Sing above storms that lash the shore.

THE OUTCAST'S DEATH.

O'ER Death's dark, chilling, deep abyss,
A soul, in fear, looked wildly down.
"As the sweet echo, down the glen,
Of waterfall long miles away,
Falls on the fainting wanderer's ear,
So come to madden heart and brain,
The loving words, passed lightly by,
From mother's, friends' and sister's lips,
So come the wrongs to trusting hearts,
The faith of youth, by my rude touch
Wakened, to learn distrust.

"Thus rose my life. A crystal spring,
With banks moss-cushioned, flower-gemmed,
O'erhung by sheltering boughs, vine-draped,
Where birds trilled back the song I sung the shore.
Clear, then, the sun threw silver on my breast,
The night threw jewels upon every wave.
So childhood's time. Years passed; the tide,
Swelled to the crest of the mossy bank,
Turned from the moan of the swaying boughs,
Laughed and leapt o'er the sentry rocks,
Swept on in speed to the plain below,
Where mile on mile the prarie glowed,
Flashing girdles of silvery streams,
Music, color and warmth o'er all.

"The crystal spring is a turbid stream;
Forest and flower throw down in scorn
Their faded robes on my struggling breast;
The drooping, sheltering evergreens,
And the pillowy bank; are far away;
The moon has wrapped her face in a cloud,
Soft and white, and the stars are gone."

The morning broke, and the sun beheld,
In its rocky bed, on the desert floor,
Hushed and frozen, the worn out stream.

TIME AND I.

I HAVE a friend, the oldest one
  Upon the record of my years,
Who, watchful how my life doth run,
  Upon its every scene appears.

Never in haste, and never late,
  Silent, yet firm, he follows me;
Though I forget, or smile, or hate
  His presence, there is he.

When but a child, with ne'er a thought
  Of him, whether to blame or praise,
Each day some newer gift he brought,
  Or woke my mind to fresh amaze.
What fairy stories then I heard
  Of wondrous things I yet should see!
Till I forgot the singing bird,
  And, wistful, left my mother's knee.

Watching life's phantoms luring on
  The eager soul through passing years,
I lost my treasures fast as won,
  Though pledged by hope, and bought by tears.
And, whether it be just or wrong
  To set such sentence in my rhyme,
The loss of youthtime, treasure, song—
  I charge it all, dear friends, to time.

And when I name him gravely so,
  It is because I can but see,
For all his vows made long ago,
  How little is fulfilled to me.
If in my glass I turn to look
  (He told me he should make me fair),
I see youth's fresh bright face he took
  And left a weary woman's there.

And, thus defrauded and denied
  Of woman's solace, as some say,
I pay a sigh to wounded pride
  And quickly look the other way.

If from my heart upswells the song
    (Time said my voice should grow more sweet),
And I my quavering notes prolong,
    My patient friends at last retreat.

Though I remonstrate 'gainst his will
    And every firm resolve declare,
'Gainst all my arts, I find his skill
    Has added silver to my hair.
And, though resigned to yield the rose
    The cheek in earlier years did wear,
I tremble now, for ah! who knows
    How soon he'll leave a wrinkle there!

Yet, though he cheat and wound me sore,
    His tyranny an end must find ;
For when I reach the other shore,
    His majesty must stay behind.
Ah! an immortal there to dwell,
    O'er loss and change no more to sigh ;
With all life's promises fulfilled,
    How blest to bid old Time, good-by!

IN SOME ONE'S ALBUM.

You say I must not partial be ;
Yes, that is true : but then, you see,
My ship of thought lies high and dry ;
Yet I'll make a wish for you and I,
Concerning our first quarrel ; 'tis,
That it may be as short as this.

THE EMIGRANT GIRL.

Its mony, mony a mile away,
  And mony a danger, too, between;
And I strive to shame, well as I may,
  The rising tears that fill my een;
But oh! I canna, canna lie
  To my ain heart, that lo'es ye true;
I canna crush the welling sigh—
  Jamie, I'm wearying for you.

The lang day's weary task is done,
  And I may sit me doon alone,
To ponder over, one by one,
  Your every loving glance and tone.
They're a' kind to the stranger girl,
  But they're na the heart that lo'es me true;
And lanely gaes the busy world—
  Jamie, I'm wearying for you.

I know ye're far and far away,
  Beyond the mountain and the tide;
But my heart gaes wi' ye a' the day,
  My footsteps follow by your side.
Oh, Jamie! hasten frae the sea,
  Back to the heart that lo'es ye true,
Ye're a' I hae that's dear to me—
  Jamie, I'm wearying for you.

THE POOR IN WALES.

DOWN the dim pathway of my dreams,
   Heard I the wail from a land afar,
Where through their woe no beacon gleams—
   I saw the homes where our loved ones are.
Pity, O parents, with firesides warm,
Sheltered safe from the raging storm.

The wail that o'er the waters came,
   Over the prairie and mountain wall,
Hath reached my heart with its human claim ;
   I cannot hush the piteous call :
"Thou art my brother in Christ, O give
Thy helping hand that we may live !

"Mothers in Zion, can ye sing
   Cradle hymns to your babies dear,
Without a pang for the perishing
   Babes on our fainting bosoms here ?
Reacheth not into your dreams, the groans
Of dying babes on the wretched stones ?"

Sleeping or waking, still I hear
   The cry and prayer of the young and old :
"Help us, O brother and sisters, dear,
   Thy praise shall be sweetest ever told."
And I heard the Spirit cry, "O send !"
And I heard the people cry, "Amen."

A PROMISE.

Mine eyes! mine eyes! rain happy tears!
For ye shall in this earthly life
Look on your Savior, on your God.
O blessed eyes! that live to-day,
Weep all your sorrow-shade away—
Ye shall look on the living Lord.
Mine eyes! mine eyes! look only up
To heaven's pure and sinless hight.
O that no vision dark, profane,
Of stain-ed earth, might intervene
To leave its blemish-touch upon
Their mirror gaze!   O, blessed eyes!
Weep happy tears! let morning's pure,
And silent night's cool, holy breath
Waft far away all earthly scenes,
For thou shalt look upon thy Christ.
O, might it be, that when His eyes
Read through mine own the heart below,
It shall be clear as crystal wave,
Through which we see the floor.

O, blessed hands! and shall ye lie
In the pure clasp of Christ's, thy Lord?
Thrill, blessed hands, with holy flame,
That Christ, the pure, the victor king
O'er mortal trial, mortal sin,
Who, unstained, passed through all we meet,
Shall look in mortal eyes and smile,
And bless thee by His own pure touch!

O, blessed hands! be pure thy touch.
O, happy feet! tread lightly on
O'er thorny paths, though weak and sore,
For ye shall tread the blessed earth
That Christ's own feet shall press upon.
O, feet, keep firm, and pure thy ways!
On dust too sacred for e'en lips
To press, your steps shall fall.

Thrill, eager heart, and brain, and ears!
Thrill, flesh and blood, and thirsting soul,
Which ne'er shall die!
For ye shall in His presence stand,
And see His face, and hear His voice.
Fear, mortal frame! lest in the light
Of His divine and beauteous eyes,
Which read all life, ye trembling fall,
And burn away beneath their glow.

EARTH-WEARY.

THROUGH heat and dust, 'till the gloom of night,
  I had wrought my task alone;
And in the strife between "might and right,"
  My spirit so weak had grown,
With eyes that drooped in the heavenly light,
  I came to the Master's throne.

Nor spake, "I am here," but, weary, laid
  My burden down at His feet,
Waiting His time; while earthward strayed
  Sad thoughts to hearts that beat
As full a life, as when I made
  My sacrifice complete.

"What hast thou brought me back, my child?"
  My heavenly Master said.
"A broken heart, all earth-defiled,
  Whence faith in human kind is fled;
Where weeds of human kind run wild,
  And heaven-lent strength is dead."

"And what hast thou with the sinful done?"
  My heavenly Master said.
"I have shunned the path of the sinful one—
  Can the blind by the blind be led?
My hand from his no stain has won,
  Nor my name a stain," I said.

"Thy Savior walked with the sinful man—
  No stain His name doth bear.
The stain which doth the sinful brand,
  A tear might wash it fair;
And if thy heart go with thy hand,
  It toucheth him as a prayer.

"And how hast thou with the lonely dealt—
  The orphan heart in thy care?
Have they the joy of thy home-life felt?
  Hast thou led them from the snare?
Had they place beside ye when ye knelt,
  And in thy love a share?

"And hath thy heart unto me stood true
  When the tempter entered in?"
"Lord, I have striven Thy will to do,
  Though oft have forgetful been,
When earthly sorrows pierced me through;
  Yet I strove Thy love to win."

"None so alone and dismayed can be
    As one who hath God forgot;
Though, bowed with grief, thou seest not me,
    Thy Master forsaketh not,
And 'mid despair my eyes shalt see,
    If ye faithful bear thy lot.

"And would ye turn from the harvest field?"
    My heavenly Master said;
"Return and toil—for I am thy shield—
    In the way thy Savior led;
Toil and rejoice in the work revealed
    For the living and the dead."

Then, while the mournful tears did rise
    For the heavenly rest denied,
I lifted up mine aching eyes—
    Lo! a curtain parted wide,
And my being thrilled with quick surprise,
    For the *dead* thronged far and wide.

They lifted their holy eyes to mine,
    In appeal more deep than speech;
And each heart-cry, by the power divine,
    To my human heart did reach;
'Till with their souls, and before His throne,
    We bowed in covenant each.

Then I cried! "I go to the earth again!
    To labor and not to mourn;
Noting no more the wrongs of man,
    For a light in my soul doth burn,
That will bless and brighten duty, 'till when
    I shall hear Him call, 'Return!'"

ESTRANGED.

And hast thou shut and locked thy heart
   Against me? Nay, not so.
Whom once I loved, I ever love;
   I cannot let thee go.
Thou, who hast dwelt within my love,
   Winning thy place so well—
Ah! must we say good by to hearts?
   I cannot say farewell.

Thou, who alone didst watch my bed
   Of sorrow, pain and fear;
While wintry night raged, dark and wild,
   And death seemed all too near.
Can I forget those dream-like days,
   When, resting in thy care,
I traced the wanderings of thy song
   Upon the charmed air!

E'en if some idle words let fall
   (As leaves float on the wind),
Long wandering, to thy gentle heart
   Its way at last did find,
Ah! who would weigh it 'gainst the past,
   With all its memories dear?
Not thou, or I, who know, so well,
   Life's holy mission here.

Ah! who would take the perfect rose,
   Love on its heart had worn,
And, counting not its loveliness,
   Treasure alone the thorn?

I could not sing in heaven, if there
   A loved face turned away,
Unreconciled; 'twould chill my joy,
   E'en in that perfect day.

Though life be long, and earth be wide,
   All vain to turn away;
We oft shall meet, amid that throng
   Who walk the narrow way.
When we shall meet beside the gate,
   Thou wilt not answer "No;"
Thou'lt know with joy my patient faith,
   For I have loved thee so.

THE WORSHIPER.

INTO the house of worship came
   The earnest, crowding throng,
The gentle girl, the aged dame;
   Through prayer, and praise, and sacred song,
To learn the path that led above
   Earth's vales and wilds of wrong.

While prayer, full-toned, sweet, clear and high,
   And worship-hymn like incense rolled,
A stranger, half as one in fear,
   To vacant seat before me stole,
Like one apart from all commune,
   Save with her secret soul.

Her garments, worn with studious care
  (The fashion of long years gone by),
The straying locks of once bright hair,
  The pallid cheek, the drooping eye,
The prayer-bent head, the shrinking form,
  Might wake a pitying sigh.

Yet, e'en as once in Eden dwelt
  One spirit dark, whose trail was blight,
There, where truth's seekers humbly knelt,
  Vain worldlings, at the saddening sight
Blushless, within the sacred place
  Their fine derision dealt.

Ah! how my soul within me burned
  To shield the helpless from their sting,
When once her thin pale face she turned,
  Then shrank like some poor hunted thing
Too weak and wounded to take flight,
  Though shouts around her ring.

Ah! what hath been thy woe, poor heart?
  What history of wrong and pain
Lie hid from reason's reach and smart?
  And but the seal-ed lids remain,
Save one stray leaf thou connest o'er,
  Thy heavenly home to gain.

*   *   *   *   *

When, low upon her dying bed,
  The lonely worshiper was found,
Few friends kind ministrations fed,
  Few mourners stood her grave around;
And the sealed lips their secret kept
  Within them, 'neath the mound.

*   *   *   *   *

Then the bright angel, lifting forth
  The poor clay from the trampled sod,
Found 'neath cankering dross of earth
  (Where worldly feet indifferent trod),
Dim with tear-rust, a jewel bright,
  Worthy the praise of God.

"Blessed thou art," the Master said,
  "Because when worldlings sought not me,
Though with my richest bounties fed,
  Thou, in thy depths of misery,
Friendless, distraught, one bright thought kept,
  And loved, and worshiped me."

THE GATES OF LIFE.

Come thou with me, my daughter dear,
  Out from these walls upbuilt by hands;
They hide, they hush, from eye and ear,
  The changing pictures of the sky,
  The endless panorama grand,
And the still voice that cometh near.

Beneath this leafy canopy,
   Lighted by rising moon and star,
Stand thou, my daughter dear, with me,
   And listen to the echo thrown
   By all the world, anear, afar,
Though on the land, or on the sea.

What is the echo thou dost hear
   In the pure silence of thy heart?
Nay, tremble not, my daughter dear,
   'Tis but the answer to His call;
   'Tis the farewell of those who part,
Of they, who, saddest, linger here.

I hear it in the city's streets,
   Below the city's mingled sounds,
And deeper, when the city sleeps;
   The sleepless mourner's piteous cries,
   Unhushed, relieve the heart's deep wounds,
In misery's dim, lone retreats.

Where goest thou, dear friend?   Alas!
   Thy heart is glad, thy hope is high;
Thou hurryest so quickly past,
   Thou seest never, before, beyond,
   How the dark tide of death flows nigh,
How it riseth, cruel and fast.

The dying maiden speaketh low
   Where lover, weeping, bends his head;
Farewell, beloved! I loved thee so;
   Forget me not, that we may keep
   These vows of earth, so vainly said,
And an immortal bridal know.

The stricken mother, mourning, bends
　Where her beloved, unanswering, lies;
All vain the love of fondest friends,
　　To soothe the heart's deep agony,
　　While memory's blessed visions rise,
And love's sweet labor hath its end.

The mother said, in tears, "I go;
　And sweet, but for the thought of thee,
The rest in death, the weary know.
　　But ah! whose loving care shall lead
　　These little ones aright, for me?
Ah, let me stay!"　Death answers "No!"

They are wending all the same, same way;
　Behold! afar o'er all the earth
The nations don their last array;
　　Listen! the mournful requiems rise
　　Up from the nations' vacant hearths,
And the wrath of God still points the way.

Listen thou! O my daughter dear!
　The roll of drums, the clash of swords,
These sounds of wailing in thine ear,
　　Change, from sad farewells, to "All hail!
　　Behold! the coming of the Lord,
Behold the reign of peace draws near!"

Listen! thrones, kingdoms tottering,
　And earth and sea all tremulous,
With thunderous voices echoing,
　　Leaping to praise their Maker's name,
　　In speech majestic tell to us,
That this is the awakening.

Beloved, 'tis not the close of life,
   Listen! these farewell cries shall change
To worship-anthems, for all strife
   Shall have an end, and, at the cry,
   All flesh shall, at the summons strange,
Fainting, awake to deathless life.

"MY SON, GIVE ME THINE HEART."

SHE rocked her baby, singing low
   Love tones that mothers sing,
To tender words that mothers know
   How fittingly to string.
And aye! the secret of her song,
   In each and every part,
Was ever, all the sweet time long,
   "My child, give me thine heart."

When nature's fairest beauties smiled,
   She loved with him to stray,
And taught the listening, trustful child,
   To fairer realms the way.
And when, amid earth's scenes of ill,
   Her anxious fears did start,
The pleading of her love, was still,
   "My child, give me thine heart."

"My child, give me thine heart;" he hears
   The heavenly Father's call;
For, fleeing to His throne, her tears
   And prayers before Him fall.

When Christ hath died that thou mightst live,
And, facing evil's dart,
   Thy mother's love no less would give,
Wilt thou withold thine heart?

Alas! how e'en Immanuel's cry
   Of desolation, pain,
Pleading for strength, with Him on high,
   While midnight hours did wane;
Fell on disciples loved, who slept,
   Though soon with Him to part;
While He in love and anguish wept,
  "Father, give me their hearts."

Alas! for him who had denied
   His Master's name and power;
Of whom e'en nature testified,
   In crucifixion's hour.
Spare me the cry of souls that wait
   The dread command—"Depart;"
Remembering at last, too late,
   "My child, give me thine heart."

WOMEN OF ZION.

WHERE fifteen hundred women thronged,*
   To answer back a listening world—
A people by their kindred wronged,
   'Gainst whom men's bitterest threats were hurled;
'Gainst whom all hearts did seem at war,
   From women at their firesides' cheer
To men whom nation's rulers are—
   I, listening, their words did hear.

---

*——Mass meeting in the Theatre, Salt Lake City, Utah, November 16, 1878.

Here, where from persecution's might
    The poor or titled exile found
A home, and did in love unite,
    And by most solemn pledges bound,
By legacy their country blessed
    With right of "life and liberty
And the pursuit of happiness"
    To their free-born posterity.

Ere yet have passed away from earth
    The last sons of that century grand,
The sacred record loses worth,
    And "might, not right," uplifts the hand.
And while scarce yet have died away
    The words our patriot grandsires spake,
Their ingrate heirs ignore to-day,
    And strive the sacred will to break.

How proud the nation's sons to pay
    Their homage to its hundred years!
And welcomed to the natal day
    The titled guests of both the spheres.
But we, the outcast heirs, must wait,
    Disowned, despised, without a voice
In her proud hall, "outside the gate,"
    While strangers at the feast rejoice.

Have patriot's children right to speak?
    Have martyr's children right to pray?
Then we, the hunted, hated, weak,
    Something in our own case may say.
Shall it count nothing unto us
    That our great grandsires fought and died
For our land's liberty, because
    Our creed from theirs may differ wide?

I saw among the multitude,
　Women from every Christian land—
E'en from the islands' solitudes,
　And from the India's heathen strands,
Who left the idol and the cross,
　Drawn by the gospel's sacred spell,
To follow Christ; nor count it loss
　To do His will, whate'er befel.

I saw, and knew the histories
　Of those who rank had laid aside,
And choosing God's high mysteries,
　With bleeding feet crossed deserts wide,
Drawing their hand-carts, day by day,
　Through wind, and rain, and bitter snows,
'Till, famine-stricken by the way,
　Their comrades' graves, like furrows rose.

Heritage of ancestral lands
　And ships at sea they counted nought,
But kneeling on the barren sands,
　Oft on dry crusts His blessing sought.
And women, driven from their own hearths,
　Fleeing before a mob's decree,
Have, 'neath the bleak sky, given birth
　To heirs of our grand liberty.

And, cradled in their wagons rude,
　Rocking o'er trackless prairies wild,
Each breathed the free air's balmy mood,
　And grew to manhood, God's own child.
And can the souls thus forged in fire
　Of outraged laws and human woes,
E'er wear the bonds of tyrants' ire,
　And all their mountain freedom lose?

Beside America's dead sea
　　Their weary pilgrimage did end;
And, in the desert's heart set free,
　　They in the red man found a friend,
And from the parched and salted ground
　　Invoked the slumbering life to wake;
And from the mountains, old and brown,
　　The hidden crystal springs to break.

Then answered to the hand of toil
　　Fair garden homes and harvest fields;
And e'en the canyon's rocky soil
　　To man her silvery treasure yields.
But scarce these blessings are secured,
　　Ere those we could not dwell among,
Ignoring all we have endured,
　　With envious eye and venomed tongue,

Survey the scene, and with well feigned
　　Sense of shocked honor, and of fear,
Issue throughout our broad domain
　　A call for holy crusade here.
But undismayed, and trusting Him
　　Who led them through the trial-path,
Though memory-pangs the eye might dim,
　　They heard God's praises in man's wrath.

Nor feared to speak, though well they knew
　　What test their words must undergo;
But strong in heart, with purpose true,
　　Their reasons for their faith dared show.
And, brave as their colonial sires,
　　Who cast aside the British yoke, .
The smouldering embers of the fires,
　　Patriot and martyr, in them woke.

And men and women, foes at heart
  To what these women dared to speak,
Heard truths that pierced them to the heart,
  And drove the quick blood to the cheek.
Remember, then, O, ye who heard
  Words Zion's daughters spake that day;
Nor hush the impulse that they stirred,
  Oppression's cruel hand to stay.

THE FLOWERS.

WINTER had wrapped his ermine robe
  Around him and was gone;
And spring, aflush with loveliness,
  Greeted the rosy dawn.

Above the hum of passing wheels
  She heard a charmed call,
And from her tired hands she let
  The weary sewing fall.
The call of nature to the heart,
  Through varied melodies,
The voice of birds and waterfall,
  And whispers of the breeze.

She left the busy, crowded town,
  And, with her child, she strayed
To where the greenwood, reaching wide,
  Its fairy haunts displayed.
She stood upon the rising hill—
  Where'er the glad eye turned,
Adown the sunny southern slopes,
  The varied colors burned.

And from the dimpled, swelling plain,
    In modest worth and grace,
Of myriad·glowing hues and forms,
    They looked up to her face.
Down from the ever-drooping boughs
    Their lovely banners hung;
And nodding bells, to passing breeze,
    Their gracious perfumes swung.

Within the forest's dewy shade
    Uprose the graceful fern;
And birds, at concert overhead,
    The brook's sweet praise returned.
And here and there she gathered them—
    These gifts of nature wild—
And all seemed giving welcome to
    The widow and her child.

Yet, o'er the gladness of the scene,
    A sacred sadness crept,
Remembering him, who once with her
    These greenwood visits kept.
And here and there she gathered them,
    And when the twilight fell,
The seamstress took back to her home
    The day's sweet rest and spell.

Then, bending o'er her treasures fair,
    For love's sweet memory,
Their beauties knew no change, transfixed
    By her rare alchemy.
And while the lovely work she wrought,
    Her heart again was young;
And long-hushed songs of happier days
    Unconsciously she sung.

Still nearer to the widow's door
    The cruel hard times pressed,
Though hard she toiled, denying self
    Of rightful food and rest.
Then spoke a neighboring widowed friend:
    "There is one, rich and great,
And she, perhaps, might buy these flowers,
    And ease your present fate."

She flushed, that aught wrought for love's sake,
    Should find a price in gold;
Yet for her child's sake, well she knew
    Her treasures should be sold.
"Now brush your daughter's sunny curls,
    And let her take them there;
And I will sit awhile with you,
    The happy news to share."
        *   *   *   *   *

She paused within the open door
    Of a rich, spacious room—
The fairest picture that it held,
    Though flowers exotic bloomed.
"What do you want! how came you here!
    I'd like to have you tell?"
"Lady," the trembling child replied,
    "I rang your front door bell;

"Your servant sent me here to you;
    Perhaps you'd like to buy
These wild-wood flowers." "How dare you come!
    Your flowers indeed! not I!
Such insolence these low, poor have!
    Right in here from the street!"
"Lady, I wiped my shoes, there is
    No dust upon my feet;

" We're poor, but we're respectable,
    We are not mean and low,
If you could see my mother once,
    You would not call her so."
Swiftly adown her flushing cheeks,
    The shining tear drops rolled,
Like loosened pearls, from broken string,
    O'er carmine velvet rolled.

She turned away with quivering lip,
    Frightened, heart-sick and sore ;
"Here !" called the haughty dame, "this way,
    Go out of my back door."
Her choking sobs she scarce could hush,
    While on the lady's ear
Fell but the sound of carriage wheels
    Of suitors, drawing near.

Ah, little need within her home,
    Her story to rehearse !
The widowed friend laid in her lap,
    The one coin in her purse.
Thou, who didst bless the widow's mite,
    Friend of the sad and poor !
Help us to still trust to Thy word,
    And all Thy tests endure.

THE GRAIN QUEENS OF ZION.

BRAVING alike the skeptic's smile
  And the near-friend's faltering faith,
Though wise ones doubt and foes revile,
  With trust no tongue can scathe.
From the city's streets and the rural lanes,
  They are gathering, side by side,
A band linked by faith's sacred chains,
  In one great cause allied.

Answering to the leader's call,
  From their gentle homes they came,
Taking the mission, one and all,
  "For love, and not for fame;"
With willing hearts and empty hands,
  The Father's aid they sought,
And, bearing out the great command,
  A wondrous work have wrought.

And they who sowed the tiny seed
  In time of peaceful harvest years,
Shall see the yield in time of need
  Bedewed by grateful tears.
Let our land boast the world-wide fame
  Of her cotton and railroad kings,
And toast in wine the princely name
  Her gold and silver brings.

Kings of the coal and iron mines,
  Each a mighty sceptre hold;
But the light of a rising power shines,
  Whose story shall be told

Unto the far ends of the earth,
　Where stricken nations bend,
Weakened with war, and plague and dearth,
　And own these as a friend.

Then, loyal daughters, who obeyed
　A noble leader's word,
Ye shall come forth, in power arrayed,
　Named, with the earth's accord,
With blessings, from the lips of those
　Saved by thy deeds of worth,
And reverence from thy fallen foes—
　The grain queens of the earth.

Then shall the gleaner's hands, though brown,
　Be blessed with truer praise
Than those born to the ruler's crown
　And idle, royal days.
Power shall attend thy given word,
　The poor may dare rely on;
And sweetest blessings ever heard,
　Crown the grain queens of Zion.

"I'M WEARYING FOR MY DAUGHTER'S FACE."

The summer moon, in silver light,
　Her fairy pictures overlaid,
Where drooping boughs and blossoms bright,
　Threw down their tracery of shade.
She sat alone, I ventured near—
　Softly beside her took my place;
She pressed my hand—"Oh! lady dear,
　I'm wearying for my daughter's face."

" 'Twas for the holy Gospel's sake
 We left Old England ; left her there
'Till we a home 'mid Saints could make,
 And she our toils and wants be spared.
Grateful, I've toiled 'till faint at night,
 But oh ! through all these lingering days,
I'm pining for the love and light—
 I'm wearying for my daughter's face.

"The good ship, bearing my dear girl,
 Comes nearer to me day by day ;
O could I watch its flag unfurl,
 And welcome her from far away !
But weary miles of this wide earth
 Stretch out between, in dreary space ;
I sit and mourn by our own hearth—
 I'm wearying for my daughter's face.

"I cannot wait for her dear feet
 To cross these mountain wilds to me ;
I must not wait, but go and meet
 The daughter dear I pine to see."
I could not answer her in speech,
 Her trembling hand I gently pressed ;
When help is far beyond our reach,
 The silent love of all is best.

For many a mile, and many a day,
 They rode, their daughter dear to meet ;
But slow for them, and long the way,
 Whose hearts with fond impatience beat.
At last, long ere the sun was down,
 They saw, below a sheltering hill,
The train had halted, gathering 'round
 Some scene, with deepest interest filled.

With courteous mien, they near and pause
  Beside the group, and greeting one
With " Welcome, Brother !" ask the cause
  Of the camp's halt, ere set of sun.
Ah ! love hath quickest ear of all !
  They hear the sweetest lips' glad cry ;
" Father and mother ! dear ones all !
  Haste to me, kiss me, ere I die !"

Ah, saddest hour that life had known !
  Ah, sweetest ! that 'twas not too late;
Their tender arms enfold their own,
  Yet cannot wrest her from her fate.
Through storm at sea, and mountain gale,
  And weary march, her courage pressed,
'Till, nearing home, she sank and failed,
  Too worn to bear joy's sweet excess.

They brought her here, that she might sleep
  With kindred faith, in holy ground;
And breaking hearts o'er her did weep,
  Who early won the martyr's crown.
And they are nearing, day by day,
  The journey's end to that far place,
To meet and clasp, and dwell alway
  In the light and love of the daughter's face.

THE BABY.

O, WHAT is all this noise about?
　The house is full of joy to-day;
I hear the laugh and call ring out—
　They cannot hear a word I say.
I cannot read, or think, or write,
　In all this racket full of fun;
I really wish that it were night,
　And they were sleepy, every one.

I don't know what I want to do,
　For hard as I may try to think,
The sound of those boot heels goes through
　My ears so sharp, it makes me wink!
And I know just how the hair I curled
　So silken smooth an hour ago,
For a rosy-cheeked, dear little girl,
　Is tossing, flying, high and low.

And baby's as wild as either one,
　The darling little household prince!
O'er racket of chairs that fall as they run,
　He shrieks with joy; I fairly wince.
Why! "The baby is walking alone to-day,"
　The first time in his little life;
Ah! the thought near takes my breath away,
　And the happy words cut like a knife.

"O! aint you proud ma'am?" Susan asks,
　"And how surprised his pa will be!"
And she forgets her crowding tasks,
　And gives him kisses two and three.

Proud? when his first steps alone
    Open my eyes to the truth, heart-sore:
He out of his babyhood has grown,
    And needs my leading hand no more.

And it seems as though the baby boy,
    I have loved so silently and well,
Must have been a dream-child, and the joy,
    The year has passed an unbroken spell.
And now, instead of a babe in my arms,
    Starting in sleep when I lay him down,
My heart is thrilled with swift alarms,
    While steady and sure, he runs around.

O my baby! to think that you
    Would choose to slide from your mother's knee;
Would rather shout with those tomboys, two,
    Than here in her loving arms to be.
When did you change, you butterfly,
    From a cradled thing to a thing of flight?
No, no, I cannot laugh while I
    Look on the new and doubtful sight.

The wide earth luring thee to go;
    Temptation's smile; ambition's call;
And thou a man! life's ways must know,
    Must meet its lessons one and all.
And I have been thy highest love!
    How weak, alas! thy mother's arms,
They cannot keep thee. Lord above,
    Lead Thou my darling safe from harm.

SO MUCH TO DO.

"O WHERE is my little daughter?
   She cannot be far away,
For only just now I heard her
   Sweet voice at her happy play."
"O! I am right here, dear mamma,
   What is it you want with me?
Only I don't think I can do it,
   I'm busy as I can be."

"Why, what in the world is't, tell me?
   What wonderful thing and new,
That my pet can't help me a little,
   When I have so much to do?"
"Why, there's so much play to be done;"
   Then added in graver way,
"And there's so much, that I don't think I
   Can finish it all to-day."

O, soul of my little daughter!
   That opened a door of light,
Though the afternoon swift was passing
   With unfinished tasks, to-night.
So busy with airy castles,
   So rich with her trifling toys,
Not counting their cost or measure,
   Content with the present joys.

No miser that counts his treasures
   So happy and restful as she,
For hers are o'erflowing and countless,
   And stainless, and bright as can be.

And she trembles not, that she may lose them,
　Nor hesitates to divide;
Nor questions the future's providing,
　For her faith, like her joy, is wide.

And so one who never read books,
　And never professed to be wise,
Has silenced my troubled spirit,
　And strengthened my weary eyes.
My day, too, is full of blessings,
　Its joys, as well as its care,
Cannot all be held in one day,
　But shall make another fair.

And I saw how e'en my own life
　Must unfinished pass to the next;
And the undone tasks around me
　No longer my spirit vexed.
And so while the birds low twittered,
　And the twilight shades fell 'round,
I'd time to spend with my dear ones,
　For my heart a rest had found.

VANISHED TOYS.

The dear little girl awaking
　Out of her balmy sleep,
As though her heart were breaking,
　Is beginning softly to weep.
O! what is this wonderful sorrow
　That shadows the darling's eyes?
And what loving art can we borrow,
　To banish the sad surprise?

Then she says, her head on my shoulder,
  While sobbing still she clings
The closer to arms that enfold her,
  "I want my beautiful things."
And unconsoled yet, though we find her
  Her treasures and dolls every one,
She weeps, looking round and behind her:
  "They were beautiful, and they are gone."

So this is the mystery, is it,
  Has conjured the grief and tear?
We were talking of Santa Claus' visit,
  And now she has dreamed he was here.
Ah! who can o'ertake us these fairies?
  These spiteful and mischievous things,
That steal even dream-toys, the rarest,
  And flit on invisible wings.

Now, auntie, don't laugh at the baby,
  For haven't we all of us known
Of dreams sent by Cupid, and maybe
  Have wakened to find they were flown?
And should some old cynic endeavor
  To prove us such dreamings are vain,
Would we, older, believe him? Oh, never!
  But listen and trust them again.

But, as she can give no description
  Of the treasures from fairy-land brought,
Nor a clue to the mystic direction
  In which the winged thieves might be sought,
Just listen a moment to mother;
  Here's an easy and beautiful plan,
And, as we know of no other,
  We'll try it as quick as we can.

Just dress her up warm in the furs
   Santa Claus brought last year,
And, wheel out that carriage of hers,
   With cushions and robes for the dear;
And take her all over the town,
   Where holiday goods are displayed,
For possibly they may be found
   Amid other treasures displayed.

And which ever the darling avers
 . Is the very same that she lost,
Be sure that the treasures are hers,
   Whatever the size or the cost.
And ah! might it ever be so,
   That waking from dreamings deep,
They may into realities grow,
   And their beauty be hers to keep.

A LEGEND.

Once, (so I heard) in some far land,
Two happy lovers wedded, and
A fairy mother to them brought
A chain of gold, richly o'erwrought
With quaint designs, and legends strange,
Befitting life in every change.

Each golden strand was made of two,
Divided oft yet linked anew.
She blessed the gift, bidding the pair
To take of it most sacred care.
And for awhile, I scarce need tell,
That all for them in life went well.

At last, (such ills will come along)
One day something with them went wrong;
And hastily one of them spoke
An unjust word.   Instantly broke
One golden link.   No mortal hand
Could mend the work from fairy land.

So ever hung before their eyes,
The broken strand, a sad surprise.
"Ah!" said the fairy, "now I fear
There's going to be trouble here;
With 'patience' broken, there are few,
Can guess how much there'll be to rue."

And sure enongh, it was not long
Before some other thing went wrong;
And judgment, without mercy sweet,
Like Shylock, urged his claim complete.
And 'neath the stress and burden hard,
The link that broke was true "regard."

Though startled, the wrong-doer sought
No angel aid, but inly thought:
"Why yield my heart to vain regret?
The strongest strands are left me yet;
Why bind the powers of my soul,
And every impulse fresh control?

"Shall I my nature free restrain?
'Love' and 'forgiveness' yet remain,
And, pure as gold, and strong as steel,
These two can bear all life can feel."
And, keeping always before view
Reliance on this anchor true.

Turned here and there, and everywhere,
The phantom joys of life to share.
Thinner and thinner grew the strands,
Upheld oft times by trembling hands.
The lovely emblems on them traced
Became, by careless use, effaced.

But never dimly shone the gold,
And still they bore a stress untold,
That heavier grew, until one day
The hand grown weakest dropped away;
Too tired to reach, one joy to keep,
Asking for naught but dreamless sleep.

And severed thus, they drifted wide:
One out upon life's restless tide,
The other silent and at peace,
Grown fairer since the soul's release,
With the safe passport to that land,
Where He mends all life's broken strands.

ANNIE'S PRAYER.

Into the "Mormon" city came
  A trader with his men;
They had heard afar its evil fame
  Repeated oft and again,
'Till fancy saw at the very name,
  A brigand-guarded glen.

No rocky walls rose to their view,
　Before the strangers' eyes
Stretched many a shady avenue
　Bedecked with the autumn dyes;
And wafts of melody sweet came through
　The air, a strange surprise.

In silence grave their seats they took
　Before the bounteous fare;
And, answering to her mother's look,
　A child offered up a prayer
Of thanks unto God ere they partook
　The bounties of His care.

Upon a man's brown cheek there burned
　A whelming tide of red,
For his soul a very truth had learned;
　And, with bent, averted head,
He rose and from the table turned,
　Soon as her prayer was said.

The gentle lady in surprise
　Followed, by pity stirred,
Fearing some illness; down from his eyes
　'Tears were falling, and she heard
Wonder-stricken, the strange replies,
　Pitying, every word:

"Lady, a stranger I came here,
　Judging you evil, all,
Walking your streets with a coward fear,
　Listening some signal call;
Watching each step that I heard anear,
　As by a foe to fall.

"When I heard in your home to-day,
  From the lips of a child,
The words of prayer, I could not stay;
  My heart was the sin-defiled,
I had strayed from the Father away;
  I was the lost and wild.

"Within my own heart I had built
  A cruel judgment seat;
In my own heart was the hall of guilt,
  And in these a temple sweet;
And the skeptic heart, with error filled,
  By a child has met defeat.

"It cannot be that he who leads
  His child by daily prayer,
Has led a life of evil deeds,
  Whatever his foes declare;
And He who the cause of justice heeds
  Will hold them in His care."

"Return," said the lady, "to the rest,
  And do not grieve you so;
You are my husband's welcome guest;
  We fear not an honest foe;
Willing are we to meet truthful test,
  And all the world to know."

SALT LAKE CITY.

ALL the valley lay in shadows,
  Cast by clouds that hid the sun;
Ripened grain fields, em'rald meadows,
  Shining lines where waters run,
Stately homes and humble dwellings,
  In their blooming foliage shrined,
Caught a charm beyond the telling,
  In the summer day's decline.

Thin as smoke-wreaths to the eastward,
  Dusky, purple mists uprolled;
Through this filmy veil, to westward,
  Softly beamed the sunset's gold;
And the while I stood in wonder,
  Silent, wrapped in fervent thought,
Lo! a rainbow crowned the splendor
  Of the picture God had wrought.

Is this lovely valley, teeming
  With all gifts from nature's hand,
The fair Zion of my dreaming,
  In the far-off golden land?
Is't the Zion, fair and holy,
  That 'neath God's own care shall rise,
Where the pure in heart and lowly
  Shall be noblest in His eyes?

Is't the Zion of those pages
   Writ by prophets grand, of old,
Who looked downward through the ages,
   And their wondrous changes told?
Is't the land where, slowly wending,
   Tribes and nations all shall meet,
In one work and worship blending,
   In one people, at His feet?

Guarded by these mighty mountains,
   Centuries thy dust has slept;
Freshened by thy wakened fountains,
   Thou to life again hast leapt.
Fair and pure as thy bright waters,
   Which no poisoned currents bear,
Rise thy countless sons and daughters,
   Royal crowns to win and wear.

Though the world now doubt the story
   Of thy sacred work and claim,
They shall live to see thy glory,
   And their fallen wreck and shame.
Though the world in hate deride thee,
   Though the waves of evil foam,
Through whatever ills betide thee,
   Thou art Zion—thou'rt my home.

Heaven-descended from a manger
   Rose thy King to victory;
Through the desert and the danger,
   He will guard thy destiny.
Brighter than the rainbow's splendor,
   Shines the crown awaiting thee,
Land of beauty! land of wonder!
   Zion, bride of Christ to be.

TO THE SPIRIT OF POESY.

SAY, where hast thou wandered, sweet spirit?
　I've missed thee for ever so long;
Thine absence and frown did I merit,
　That I've waited in vain for thy song?
Did I wrong thee when, leaning beside me,
　I slighted thy voice in mine ear?
Did I grieve thee, in that I denied thee
　My homage when last thou wert near?

Nay! take it not so, for thou knowest
　In my heart there is none like to thee;
That I'm doubly alone when thou goest,
　Withdrawing thy pleasure from me.
'Tis pity enough to be weary
　With duties that crowded the day;
Think how lonely the evening, and dreary,
　When I find thou hast flitted away!

Through each homely and practical duty
　Thou knowest impatient I haste,
To spend in the spell of thy beauty
　The moments too precious to waste.
Ah, surely thou wilt not forsake me!
　Mine eyelids are weary for sleep;
If I rest me awhile wilt thou wake me,
　Thy promise and visit to keep?

Forget not how happy we've wandered
　Through scenes still to memory dear;
How thy whispers of hope I have pondered,
　Till their soothing has banished the tear.

And how shall I go on without thee?
  No scene, be it ever so rare,
But I'd miss thy sweet presence about me,
  Thy rapture and praises to share.

Nay, thou art not gone altogether—
  For hast thou not vowed, dearest friend,
Whatever the way or the weather,
  To keep by my side to the end?
I can but believe thou art near me,
  My trial to witness and test;
I entreat thee, again let me hear thee,
  I'll honor thy slightest request.

Still silent?   I know now thou'rt hiding;
  'Twas thy presence I felt, I am sure.
Ah, well, if I merit thy chiding,
  Thy sternest I'll patient endure.
No answer!   Perhaps 'tis to tease me;
  'Twould relieve thee, to chide me, if vexed;
I'd rather do penance, if't please thee,
  Than linger so sorely perplexed.

Let me sing! perhaps music may move thee
  Of thy humor capricious to tire;
Thy favorite song soon shall prove thee—
  Ah! where hast thou hidden my lyre?
No hand but thine own can have taken
  The harp that thou gavest to me;
No other its music can waken,
  Unless they have helper in thee.

Return me thy gift, gentle spirit,
  No longer in silence to bear,
But to use, and that they who shall hear it,
  Its heavenly worth may declare.
And leave me no more, I implore thee;
  Sing with me, and teach me to sing,
Till the hearts of the hearers before thee
  Their tributes of homage shall bring.

TROPHIES TAKEN IN LOVE'S WARFARE.

INDEED, I don't know why 'tis so;
  Really, I'm not by nature vicious;
But surely as I open this,
  I'm bound to feel a spark malicious.
This little rosewood desk don't look
  As though it held aught out of reason,
And yet the sight inspires my soul,
  As though I'd caught a scent of treason.

Within this perfumed satchel's fold,
  Serenely lie some dainty letters;
Such pearly paper, golden edged,
  Many a time I've read their betters.
And yet with them I would not part;
  The reason why I most enjoy them:
The unrequited asked me once,
  To please return or else destroy them.

Here is a volume, choice indeed!
    The giver was, in mien, distinguished,
And held himself in such reserve,
    That modest men felt quite extinguished.
'Twas proffered with so grave an air,
    It seemed of his own mind, the reflex;
Until I learned, by accident,
    He knew the contents by the index.

Ah, mute and faded, poor rosette!
    Let me record the wearer's story:
He left the college halls, to tread
    The noisy fields of war and glory.
And did his fair cheek paler turn
    When hosts with wrong and death were grappling?
No! he, to guard his country's flag,
    Had enlisted as a chaplain.

Here is a poem, sweetest thing
    Ever by poet mad indited.
You well might deem so exquisite
    A heart, denied its love, were blighted.
Yet from his soul's poetic fire,
    My own no kindred flame could borrow;
He went away, resolved to be
    The hero of a lofty sorrow.

This fairy shell to me was brought
    From somewhere off the coast of China,
Inviting me to be first mate
    To the brave captain of the *Nina*.
An ocean life I could not brave,
    And now my rover of the billow
Rests his fair head, in dreamings deep,
    Serenely on a wedded pillow.

Here are some withered woodland flowers,
   That grew where paths were softly shaded—
A pretty place—and my pet deer
   Along the stream beside us waded.
We thought alike on all things but
   Our faith (he said that I was blinded),
And I regretted one so good
   Could be so very narrow-minded.

This oak leaf tells where once I stood :
   The golden sunlight o'er us sifted,
And perfumes sweet, from orchard blooms
   And clover meadows, by us drifted.
The handsome farmer's earnest face,
   With worthy, honest pride was burning ;
Those cows, that looked so picturesque,
   Set me to thinking of the churning.

This shining star, some years ago,
   Adorned the shoulder of a major,
So wise and lucky, it was said,
   He'd ne'er been known to lose a wager.
"All's fair in love and war," 'tis said ;
   But he who plans a calculation,
Should guard his sortie well, lest he
   Should lose, not win, a decoration.

And is this all? Well, you might say,
   No other token here lies hidden,
And yet unto my secret heart,
   Here is another, all unbidden!
This odor rare of violet,
   As fresh, as sweet to-day as ever,
Whispers to me, with perfumed breath:
   Love never dies, but lives forever!

When I recount the siege of years,
    When Cupid's generals besieging
The citadel that's called the heart,
    By sorties open and intriguing,
The flags of truce so oft unfurled
    (Each with a mental reservation,
To haul it down and float the flag
    Of victory and usurpation),

I fain would give a parting thrust
    At these retreating, gallant foemen ;
Ah, well! I took some banners, and
    That ought to satisfy a woman.
Such wounds as I may have received,
    Were not beyond the power of healing,
And might have been forgotten, but
    For these, the past to me revealing.

'Tis pleasant to remember that
    The accoutrements were all befitting
The cause, whether in ball rooms' glare,
    Or in the fairer moonlight sitting.
Though in the rural walks or rides,
    Or gliding o'er the silvery water,
The bow and lance were new and bright,
    And ready for the bloodless slaughter.

The fading light reminds me that
    The sun has set and twilight's falling ;
And I must close my desk and go,
    For voices sweet and dear are calling.
And ah! might every woman true,
    Love's warfare done, in peace discover,
Honor in every victory,
    And life-long friend in every lover.

MORE FLOWERS.

FROM out my scanty garden
  Shut in by high brick wall,
I gathered for my Caroline,
  One cluster, that was all.
O'erjoyed awhile she singing strayed,
  And then this pet of ours
Came gently, wistfully: "Dear ma,
  My hand would hold more flowers."

I could not help the sudden tear
  By her sweet plea evoked,
Nor bar out memory's pictures true,
  This one poor blossom woke.
I thought of meadows far away,
  Where I, in childhood's hours,
Played, listening to the wild bird's song,
  And filled my lap with flowers.

Of giant trees with vines o'erdraped,
  Of streams where wheels were set;
And tangled berry thickets, where
  The birds and children met.
Of willows high, with grape-vine swings,
  Where I, all unafraid,
Rocked, listening to the chorus grand
  The sweeping tempest played.

Of sunny slopes, where strawberries
  Lay ripe for eager hands,
And farther back, where lovely shells
  Lay on the shining sands.

I thought how all my early paths
    Were decked at every turn
With beauties fresh,, from which the heart
    Some lesson pure might learn.

I thought of how the Father's love
    Had scattered, far and wide,
Blossoms of every kind and hue,
    O'er vale and mountain side.
And yet, from all that bloom and die
    Beneath the smiling sun,
Ungathered and unpraised, my pet
    Had but this single one.

I tell her that the earth is fair,
    And yet, before her eyes,
Unsightly buildings crowd and lean,
    And clouds of dust uprise.
And when I speak of sweet sounds heard
    In some farm-home retreat,
How can she understand, 'mid sounds
    That fill a city's street?

Yes! for her sake, life's earnest dreams
    I must awhile forego,
And gather beauties 'round our home,
    That I would have her know.
And, though the song within the heart,
    Silent in mine remain,
If it be heard though her young life,
    'Twill be the mother's gain.

CHILDHOOD'S HOME.

My childhood's home! There's a holy spell
That no power can break; no tongue can tell
What a whelming tide of joy comes back
Over the rugged memory-track.
How fair was that home! There the lilac threw
O'er the porch its sprays of palest blue;
The jessamine climbed 'round the cottage door,
And starry blossoms threw on the floor;
The bees hummed low in the crowding flowers,
The birds sang loud in the grapevine bowers;
And butterflies glanced in the warm bright sun,
From morning light, 'till the day was done.

I shall see it never again;
Time with his scythe has busy been;
Even if I could go, to-day,
To that childhood's home so far away,
I should see it with lonely eyes—
Tears for the loved and lost would rise.
Those skies may be as blue to-day,
But childhood's tresses have turned to gray.

I should follow with weary feet,
Where once I led, with footsteps fleet.
Every tree would a witness seem
Of those bright days, and their blest dream,
Too rudely broken; they would bring
To mind the songs we used to sing.
Ah, why should melodies live on
When lips that made them sweet are gone?

No, no, dear home! let memory,
Or sleep, recall thy scenes to me;
And the fair pictures will awake
A sense of joy and peace, and make
My spirit glad and strong once more,
And failing aims of life restore.

VIOLET.

This violet perfume as it floats
In subtle fragrance 'round my head,
Calls back a misty memory
Of one sweet, odorous summer day,
When flowers yielded their perfume
To zephyrs, throbbing with bird notes,
And tune of cooling waterfalls,
And glimpses through the fleece-white clouds
Of that blue heaven which ne'er had veiled
Its peace serene o'er my young life.

How sweetly comes the picture back!
So fair, so true, sweet memory!
The calm, smooth landscape, stretching on
Down from the mountains to the sea.
Within the curtain-hung alcove
A dainty table faced the sun;
And you and I turned over leaves
Of poets' thoughts, or pictures fair;
Or you to me the history told
Of some rare scene from far off land.

And reading this, or viewing that,
Or listening what your tongue might tell,
I noted vaguely (yet stayed not
To turn and question whence it came)
An odor floating softly, as
Though evading to awake
My spirit to its presence sweet.

At last, perplexed, I turned and looked,
To catch the subtle, luscious charm,
Yet found it not.   Through afternoon,
Down into fading sunset hour—
Whence came the odor? here, then gone!
And turning quick, I caught, in act,
The gentle ministrant of all;
For in your careful hand, dear friend,
So quietly, a jewelled, rare,
Gold fretted phial, dropped upon
My shoulder its rare flower-heart wealth.

How like thy life in every part!
Through passing years so true, so fond;
So quietly, so sweetly, ever
Your spirit ministered to me
Its wealth of faithful, earnest care.

Across the years of silence cold,
This floating perfume comes, and brings
The phantoms of that far off time.
Dead lie the shadows of the past,
Only their beauty comes to me,
And 'neath the spell my soul returns
To live again its early dreams.

ON THE PORTRAIT OF A COUNTESS.

SUCH a portrait as we read of,
In the Old World o'er the waters,
In the countries where hearth-hist'ries
Intertwine with fate of kingdoms,
Ladies' jewels and men's armors,
Palace fetes and battle tents;
Where the flower-white hand waved farewells,
And where, looking from high turret
Or low kneeling in the twilight,
Praying for the plumed hero
(Lying dead beneath the shadows;
All forgetful of earth maiden),
Who 'mid throng and mirth, fill lightly
Days and hours that must be borne
Ere the war is ended; or the
Page comes far with loyal message
To the rose-crowned ball room queen.

So, I fancy, stood the lady,
Proud, uncaring for the homage
Hearts all 'round her thronged to proffer;
Looking past them to that far field
Where, in her thought, rode on proudly
Conqueror of field and heart;
Wearing in the heart-deep eyes, too,
(As the bordering forest branches
Float soft shadows on sunned praries,)
Somewhat of a chidden fearing,
'Mid her pride, for his proud daring.

Much like this ran through her hist'ry,
This proud lady from the Old World,
Who, for faith, from her land exiled,
Oft has charmed me with her story.
But the while her voice's pathos
Wrought its sep'rate far off spell,
From the words her lips were telling,
I've listening, dreaming, pondered
On her portrait 'gainst the wall.

Such a face as those we read of:
Wealth of hair whose sheen was purple,
And the low brow artists love;
Eyes whose will reflected in them—
I have wondered what their beaming
In the season when love veiled them;
For before the artist's coming,
Restless spirit fashioned in them
The expression that he copied—
Oh the face was fair to see!
Such a face as all men love,
And have drawn the shining sword for;
For the winning and possessing
Of the hand, drooped like a lily,
And the cheek whose color, glowing,
Lit up flame in mail-ed bosoms;
And the neck whose regal beauty
Stilled the spirit into silence,
As in dreams that charm and rouse us,
Sleep, the dreamer holdeth still.
And the while I sit and ponder,
Runs her voice's music on,
And my heart might feast between them,

Rising yet to other dreams;
But her lips breathe forth in accents
Somewhat sadder, also fonder—
His name—and I, waking, turn.

AUNT CLARE.

You toy, dear, with this little chain,
And twine it 'round your finger tips,
Your dainty, rosy finger tips,
With so unconscious, absent smile;
You only see a golden chain.

Ah me, dear! twenty years ago,
I then was twenty, old enough
To know life's true hearts, old enough
To tire of conquest, and would fain
Have trusted one of years ago.

But, blame me not. We may not all
Do that which we would wish to do,
The duty which 'twere sweet to do;
For circumstance may warp the life,
As plain to us as 'tis to all.

And we must do and bear the blame,
Nor speak, nor show our wounded feet,
Our paining, faltering, weary feet;
Show not the thorns we tread upon,
But hear, nor seem to hear the blame.

Henri first loved me; from old Spain,
He, brave and travel-browned, came home,
And brought his good ship, *Sea Bird*, home,
Laden with many a curious thing
Brought from the shores of proud old Spain.

And I, of all the wondrous store,
Took one quaint shapen piece of gold,
A nature-shapen piece of gold,
Just as it came from its dark bed
In earth's deep hidden, silent store.

And pleasantly the days passed on,
Then Henri asked me for his bride;
And worthy he, a fairer bride,
And, though I knew his worth, I wept,
And sad for both, the days passed on.

And then he went to other lands,
To come no more. I knelt and prayed:
"Bless, comfort, guard him, Lord," I prayed
Through many a month. Then came the word
Of Henri's grave in far off land.

Then Gerald loved me, and to him
I gave my heart and told him all,
And of Henri's gift I'd kept through all;
He took and fashioned this little chain,
I wore it for Henri and for him.

O! noble and tender the love he gave,
And pure and fair as his perfect face!
And my life's each day, wore but his face
On its tablets white, save now and then
A memory shade that Henri's gave.

Then Gerald, too, went out to sea;
My wrung heart uttered not its moan,
But every night the sea's sad moan
Crept through the dark, and told of storms
That lashed that frail, lone bark at sea.

And one night, dark the sun went down;
The mad sea thundered forth its wrath;
The sea-birds fled before its wrath,
From the rocky cliffs that trembled too,
And, hovering, shrieked as that ship went down.

To you alone its story's told;
And may you never weep as I,
And should you meet one, lone, as I,
Think over in your quiet heart,
The sad, true tale Aunt Clare has told.

THE TRIUMPH.

A MOTHER sat with her boy alone,
    Within her quiet room;
A tender silence 'round them hung,
    A spirit as of gloom.
"My son, wilt thou amend this wrong?"
    Her loving tones were vain;
Though pleading with him true and long,
    No answer could the mother gain.

Unseen by both, but on either side,
　A spirit, watching, stood;
And one was dark and evil-faced,
　And one was fair and good.
And when the son in silence bowed
　His head in stubborn shame;
The evil angel's face was proud,
　The victory of wrong to claim.

And, turning to the angel fair,
　With mocking smile he said:
"What record does your tablet bear?"
　The fair one turned his head
Aside, to hide the falling tears,
　Yet answered him with truth:
"Naught, but her prayers my Master hears,
　And He will save the youth."

O'er every chord in the erring heart,
　A mother holds the key;
And, He who saw the mother's tears
　Hath helped the victory.
Swiftly, his tablet's record, bright,
　The fair one heavenward bore;
But the dark one's face was lost to sight,
　And was seen again no more.

THE WANDERER'S SONG.

'TIS all that we have left of him,
  The plaintive song he used to sing;
The heart grows sad, the eye grows dim,
  And memory, yet will, waking, cling
Around our broken hopes and faith,
Of early joys, the mournful wraith.

Oft times its tender spirit steals
  Across some passing, lonely hour;
Again, the past unto me yields
  Its vanished scenes, with living power;
Again, I mourn with him who plead
With song, for love, when love was dead.

How the sweet story of the song
  Foreshadowed his life's mystery!
The bright, the sweet, the gloom, the wrong,
  Fulfilled in his own history;
Ah! still for love, for him it pleads,
For the far wanderer intercedes.

Though far off scenes have lured away
  The boy to manhood's freedom grown,
Within the hearts at home, alway,
  His name hath place, though years have flown.
'Tis in the heart, though hidden long,
And wakens at the dear one's song.

ROB EARLIE.

Aye! he will leave her widowed home,
　He's going across the sea,
Through rich and foreign lands to roam,
　When he comes back, sae grand to be.

But aye she moans, and aye she weeps,
　"I care na for the gold ye'll gain,
The treacherous winds hide 'neath the deep,
I ne'er may see your face again.

"And wha'll care for your mither, Rob,
　When simmer's gane wi' a' her store,
And winter winds are wailing, Rob,
　Wi' cold and famine, at her door?

"And wha shall cheer her lonely hearth
　Wi joyfu' song and mony a tale,
While ye, wha kens, whaur o'er the earth
　Your weary wandering steps may fail?"

But soft he smoothed her thin gray hairs,
　And soft he wiped away her tears:
"For my ain Jean sae true, sae fair,
　And you, wi' a' your loving fears,

I gae, wi' heart sae glad and light,
　To stranger lands, whaur toil may claim
The yellow gold, the siller bright,
　To mak ye baith a happy hame."

　　　*　　*　　*　　*　　*

And often at her open door
  When simmer's twilight soft hung 'round,
Wi' lips that muttered o'er and o'er:
  "The ship was wrecked, and he was drowned,"

Dame Earlie sat wi' folded hands;
  And nane that heard, but pitying wept,
To hear her tales o' foreign lands,
  And the cruel coast whaur Robbie slept.

And Jean wi' a' a daughter's care,
  A gentle care to her did gie,
Through mony a year—'till frae above,
  Ae night, ae face sae fair to see,

Peered in upon her as she lay
  Sae calm asleep, nor woke her rest;
And Jean, when rose the smiling day,
  Cam in and found the empty nest.

        *   *   *   *   *

And, sitting in her quiet room,
  Through winter evenings lone and dim,
Sae prayerfu' toned, up through the gloom
  Floats on the air, some sweet kirk hymn.

Ae manly face beneath the deep,
  Ae broken heart beneath the sod;
She's weary too, for life's last sleep,
  And only waits the time o' God.

A CHRISTMAS STORY.

"FATHER, my cousins came to-day
  And wanted me to go
And spend with them the Christmas time,
  If you would grant it so.
Teams will be passing all the day,
  Some one will let me ride;
I'd gladly walk there, every step,
  But for the river wide."

He took the black pipe from his lips,
  And turning in his chair,
Scanned with dull look, the figure small,
  Patiently waiting there.
"I never cared for holidays,
  And if the day is good,
I shall go to the canyon, sure,
  On Tuesday, to get wood.

"Still, you may go on Monday, girl;
  Tuesday will Christmas be,
But you must be beside the shore
  At sundown, waiting me."
Grateful, she, singing, brought the wood
  In, through the dark and snow,
And built the fire to warm the room,
  And cheer him with its glow.

Around the old log house that night,
   The winter winds roared wild;
But never thought of fear crept in
   The glad dreams of the child.
And when the morning's work was done,
   She dressed with happy pride;
And friends soon passing to the town,
   Gave the poor child a ride.

And never in some grander sphere,
   Was guest more welcome met;
And each hour as it glided past,
   Found her still happier yet.
When bedtime came, they, merry, hung
   Her stocking with the rest,
And wondered if old Santa Claus
   Would know she was a guest.

But crowning triumph over all
   The Christmas table seemed;
Such luxuries the town affords,
   In country homes ne'er dreamed.
But, swift descending from this hour,
   The afternoon went on,
Until the clock reminded her
   The day would soon be gone.

The loving farewells quick were said,
   Her hood and scarf she tied,
And, hurrying lest she kept him there,
   She reached the river side.
Far up and down she looked in vain,
   Nor team, nor horseman near;
Yet to the happy home behind
   Dare not return for fear.

Shallow in winter, in its bed,
    The frozen Weber lies;
Yet, from the sunshine of the day,
    It had begun to rise.
She looked upon the sinking sun,
    Which road, she scarce dared choose;
Then forced by fear, sank on the snow
    And stripped off hose and shoes.

It was not high—scarce to the knee
    Uprose the turbid flood;
Yet broken ice that drifted by,
    Like arrows pierced her blood.
Benumbed, she climbed the miry bank,
    And tried her hose and shoes,
But the wet feet and aching hands
    The needful act refuse.

Frightened and chilled, she stood alone,
    And now the sun was down;
The rising wind began to moan
    And evening shades to frown.
Then, lest they hide the lonelier path
    That from the highway led,
With one prayer-cry to Him who sees,
    The poor child turned and fled.

Cruel, the river's icy flood;
    Cruel, the drifting snows;
She scarce could tell, as on she ran,
    If her feet burned or froze.
Sobbing, the suffering child pressed on,
    When upward through the night,
Dim twinkling through the driving storm
    She saw their window's light.

Alone, before their glowing fire,
  The foster parents sat,
Plain bounteous fare the table filled,
  And hark! "What sound was that?"
He opened slow, the heavy door,
  'Gainst it the storm had piled
A foam-white bed—the sleeper is
  Their poor adopted child.

"William," the frightened woman cried,
  "I knew it would be so!
I told you that she would be there,
  And wanted you to go."
They broke the sleep so like to death,
  And while the mother lives,
The sweetest words of memory 'll be,
  "I know you—and forgive!"

THE DRUNKARD'S WIFE.

DAYLIGHT is past, and twilight at last
  Is shadowing hill and vale,
And the fair full moon, though gathering gloom,
  Is rising clear and pale.

The winds go by with a hurried sigh,
  And the stars look coldly down;
The moon rays fade, and night's dull shades
  Hide from me the dreary town.

The tale seems old, when we hear it told,
  Of the sorrow that wine can bring;
The tale is true, and the sorrow is new
  To each heart where it clasps and stings.

The stars are as bright in the heavens to-night,
  As though sorrow never had been;
And the shades that fall, close 'round like a pall
  'Round the deep sins of dark-souled men.

But the shouts go up, 'round the foaming cup,
  To be borne on the night's cold breath;
'Till wearied they sleep; while women must weep,
  For the woe, aye! dark as death.

A PICTURE.

OLD, and withered and gray!
  From my window I see her pass,
And fancy follows the stranger's way,
  And I see, in the poet's glass,
The visions of life's brighter day,
  The record of her past.

Old, and withered and gray!
  Who once hath been a winsome child,
Ready to turn from her joyous play
  At her mother's call, with a smile;
Whom angels loved as she knelt to pray,
  With heart all undefiled.

Old, and withered and gray!
　Who once hath been a cherished bride,
When life was new, and bright the way;
　With one brave and true beside,
To walk hand in hand with her alway,
　Across the world so wide.

Old, and withered and gray!
　Yet once smiled up into her eyes
A babe who had laid aside the ray
　Of his spirit's crown, to win a prize
On earth; to gain o'er sin the sway,
　Immortal then to rise.

Old, and withered and gray?
　The Father does not call her so,
With whom eternity is as a day,
　And whose hair is white as snow;
And who marked for her the devious way,
　Her trembling feet must go.

Old, and withered and gray!
　The failing senses each and all,
Are shutting out sights and sounds of day,
　As softly as a curtain's fall;
And, yielding back these joys of clay,
　She, patient, waits His call.

Old, and withered and gray,
　Her trembling steps nearing the grave,
She hears the welcoming angel say:
　"Faithful and pure, and true and brave,
Thou hast wrought thy task, hast filled thy day,
　Hast conquered, and art saved."

GRANDFATHER.

HERE is the little gray house by the street,
  With the great apple tree shading the end,
Here, underneath it, is grandfather's seat,
  Where he would sit while his ropes he would mend.

The door is ajar; come in friends and sit down.
  Here is the corner where grandfather slept,
Where so softly the presence of death fell around;
  We scarce could believe, though around him we wept.

Here is the pathway, made smooth for his steps,
  Where his steps softer fell than the sound of his cane;
Here yet, may his spirit walk by us perhaps,
  But falt'ring no longer, and free from all pain.

And so softly he went, and such peace with us left,
  And in death wore the beauty long years had laid by,
That death looked like joy; and the heart, though bereft,
  Could not feel that 'twas cruel, when thus he could die.

Here is the clock, and I cannot but turn,
  When it strikes, for his face, and his "What is the time?"
Grandfather is now where the golden light burns—
  Days turn not to night, in that heavenly clime.

Grandfather cared not for books and deep lore,
  But his life owned the peace that a king could not claim;
And he knew the deep sea, and perhaps had learned more,
  On its bosom, of trust in the Holy One's name,

Than many a one out of colleges turned,
　Who studied for fashion and orator's fame;
But grandfather's lore by observance was learned,
　And the pride of his life was an honest man's name.

And God had been good to him—gave to him all
　Of years he desired, that with plenty were filled;
So, contented, he waited the angel to call
　The soul that was ready to go when God willed.

Grandfather never professed to be wise;
　But I find myself wondering if, when I go,
My life will as faultless be, 'neath judgment eyes,
　As grandfather's record in that time will show.

Grandfather's gone! and before us has gained
　Station and name in that higher, pure band;
We've a friend there to meet us and greet us again,
　When we come to the gate of the beautiful land.

GRANDMOTHER.

"Isn't grandmother beautiful?"
　Questioned a little child,
That, as she waited an answer,
　Looked up to me and smiled;
A smile with never a shade
　Of doubt in its love expressed;
While the sweet voice, more fond than words,
　The dear old name caressed.

Beautiful, when the eighty years
　　Their furrows deep had made
On brow and cheek, and on her hair
　　Their faded lines had laid?
Beautiful, when the aged form,
　　By cruel accident,
And years of patient suffering,
　　To strangest shape was bent?

Yes, beautiful! the grandchild's sight
　　Pierced through the livery
Of earth-wrought thrall, to where the soul
　　Shone free from misery.
She understood the nature true,
　　Beneath the homely guise,
And met, with answering love, the look
　　That lit the fading eyes.

If I might choose one picture rare,
　　Of beauty, love and truth,
'Twould be these two, if brush could paint
　　The charm 'twixt age and youth.
The years have passed—grandma is gone;
　　From out my memory,
I take thy filial words, dear child,
　　And weave these lines for thee.

MINNIE.

Beautiful! so beautiful!
  In form and face and mind,
Around her spirit, the group of home
  Their hearts' best love entwined.
Within her blue eyes shadows
  Of love and pity crept,
And o'er her cheeks the impassioned glow
  Of earnest feelings swept.

The hand, so childlike, bravely
  Bore charity's sweet gift,
And the timid feet, through dark or storm,
  Sped light and sure and swift.
Why was it? just as we've seen
  Through heaven's tranquil blue,
The sudden lightnings rift the sky,
  Like arrows driven through,

Ere scarce had dawned her morning,
  So woe, and fear, and blight,
'Round them have swept their cruel storm
  And sorrow's deepest night.
But gentle as one resting,
  Half waking, half a-dream,
She lay, forgetting time and pain,
  As flowers drift down a stream.

Then over the morning still,
  Came sound of Sabbath bell,
And so, wistfully, she turned to hear
  The pealing chorus swell.
"I shall not long be with you,—
  O, mother! mourn not so,
I've done nothing wrong in all my life,
  And I'm not afraid to go.

"It is your place, dear mother,
  By grandma's side to be ;
If there isn't room beside you, make
  A place at the foot for me.
And let it be on Sunday,
  While the church bells ring ;
They'll miss me here, but my soul will be
  Far heavenward journeying.

"And don't forget the old folks,
  Don't let them miss my care,
And mother, give all my things away,
  That I never more shall wear ;
And when the holidays come,
  Oh! don't forget the poor—
I never felt well 'till they had theirs—
  Dear mother, O, do be sure.

"I may not tell all I've seen,
  But they're waiting for me here ;
I've seen so much that I want to go,
  And you'll soon come, mother, dear."
She turned her face, and sleep awhile
  Its gentle silence shed,
Then wakened to call her mother's name,
  Who, answering, kissed the dead.

What shall they do without her
 So quickly snatched away,
Who was the light, and love, and hope,
 But cold and gone to-day?
What shall they do? One only
 Can answer, for He holds
His fairest jewels in His safe hands,
 While searching all our souls.

When shall they see her? Blessed
 The promise that God gives:
That each may win to himself again
 The boon for which he lives!

A LITTLE SONG.

THERE is a song, a tender song,
 Its words are veiled in foreign tongue,
But on its cadence floats along
 The sweetest burden ever sung.

I know not what its words may be,
 But oh! I know the music's power;
How sweet! how deep! its charm for me
 Will haunt my heart forever more.

This little song of a fair clime
 One voice unto my ear hath taught;
My heart-strings thrill beneath its chime,
 That voice with sweetest magic fraught.

No other song, no other voice,
    Hath e'er such charming in its tone;
It bids my spirit, faint, rejoice,
    Yet chimeth with life's saddest moan.

O tender heart! that holds the song,
    O tender voice! that makes the spell;
I know the many thoughts that throng,
    The words that lips will never tell.

And when hereafter you will sing,
    Through twilight, wafts of song and hymn,
.This one will come and with it bring
    A memory, though faint and dim,

Of far-gone, pleasant summer days;
    You'll think of one who once was here,
Wand'ring content 'mid rural ways,
    To whom this little song was dear.

PARINTHA'S RIDE.

THE fiery sun throughout the day,
Had burned the moisture cool away
From underneath the vine-draped tree;
Had met the salt breeze from the sea,
Which, when it came, hot, stifling,
The drooping verdure withering,
Was worse than the still heat before;
While faint and far, the ocean's roar
Came, now and then, like Nature's groan,
Sorrowing deeply and alone.

As sank the day in its own heat,
We heard afar, like muffled beat
Of drums, the storm-king's thunder-call.
High! low! the lightning's flash and fall,.
The winds rise high, the tree writhes wild
In the storm-fiend's grasping, like a child.
I watch its fury rage and die,
Leaving a dull, gray, vacant sky,
So still, so passionless and pale—
Why should it 'mind me of a tale
So like the day's fierce storm, and then
Without its calm at eve again?

She was one of three sisters fair,
Alike blue-eyed and sunny-haired;
One older, taller, graver grown,
One younger, fairer, merrier toned;
Scarce more than child, whose heart as yet
Only its home-world life had met,
But she, a something strange did bear,
Like a crown's shadow on her hair,
As hidden violets' sweet perfume,
Reveal their presence in the room.

Not always rested on her face
The mystic, spiritual grace;
Oft times as careless as e'er played
The idle wind, the changeful shade;
Oft times as joyous as a child,
Her nature, uncontrolled, ran wild
Through every phase of happiness;
So earnest, yet all artlessness,
Like flight of bird lost to the sight,
Or cascade's leap from dizzy height,

'Till by some swift look, tone, or word,
(Like echoes in some lone path heard)
She startled in the heart, a thought
Of fear for her, who faltered not.

They who best knew her, wond'ring smiled,
"When will these moods have end, dear child?
These ways that, spite of grave intent,
Convert us to thy merriment;
To leave our thought, or book, to trace
The swift expressions of thy face;   *
Enwrapped so, waking only when
Thou art thy proper self again.
Wond'ring afresh, when riseth through
Thy brow's white calm, thine eye's clear blue;
The nameless something, that upholds
Itself in view, yet 'neath control."

"Sea bird," "Skylark," and "prairie wind,"
Such names, to fit such moods they'd find;
But when the revel-hour was o'er,
They belonged to her white face no more.
Again, how royal seemed her tread!
How rare, the golden, curl-crowned head!
Love framing, as she passed anear,
Expression fond; and where so e'er
The grandeur of her presence fell,
The name, Parintha, sounded well.

Oft times her father's hand was laid
In reverent love upon her head:
"My daughter, thou must never go
From us, less tender love to know.

The World's breath o'er thy heart strings will
Breathe harsher music, that would chill
Thy smiles to tears, thy light to shade;
Thy young life's joys in wreck be laid.''

One summer, when the sun came down
With fiercer rays, they left the town.
Where the Sierras high uprose,
Matching the white clouds with their snows;
With scarce a sound, beside the call
Of mountain bird and waterfall;
With moss to hush the wanderer's tread,
And glimpse of heaven's blue o'er head;
Here, in pure nature's fair retreat,
She her life's destiny did meet.

And she for love's own sake did bear
His name, and lot; and with him share
A life of solitude, apart
From peopled streets and halls of art.
Far in an oasis he built
Their home, and her sweet presence filled
Its rooms with pictures rare beyond
The artist's making, still or fond.
And music, when she sang or spake,
The desert's olden spell did break,
For seldom, o'er the desert road,
The stranger came to their abode;
But men who rode fleet as the wind,
Where stranger, path nor pass could find,
Who'd die for her, who'd die with him,
Both guard and servant, dwelt with them.

One morn, ere sunrise shafts of flame
Waked them from sleep, a rider came,
Dusty and faint; for all the night
He had ridden beneath the dim starlight:
"Our two best horses, saddle in haste!
There is no time in words to waste;
The Mexicans have taken him,
And granted all he asked of them.
They will spare his life 'till the sun goes down,
And will wait and watch, outside the town."

Nor cry, nor tear, her woe betrayed;
Lifting her child from where it laid,
She wrapped it 'round and closely pressed
Its sleeping face unto her breast;
While white-faced men in mute amaze
Upon her saint-like features gazed.
And while befitting words they sought,
Of fear, for her who faltered not,
Without a farewell word or look,
Her horse's bridle rein she took;
Stroked his long mane, leapt to her seat,
Kissed thrice her sleeping baby sweet,
Spoke to her steed; he leaped ahead
And in the race for life they led.

Down from their rocky, shady glen;
Out from the sight of wondering men,
Whose lips no helping word could say,
But in their hearts for her did pray.
Past where the little streamlet ran
And sank amid the burning sand,

Where neither tree nor rock uprear
To cast a shade; but dull and drear,
Mile upon mile on every side,
The hungry desert stretches wide.

Silent, hour after hour they rode,
Higher and fiercer the high sun glowed;
'Till sky and sand each seemed to meet
In quivering arrowy lines of heat;
And the cactus' glowing colors vie
With the richest hues of the sunset sky.

They rode where never a bird doth wing
Its homeward flight, nor living thing,
Save the horned snake, and horned toad,
Are found along the desert road;
Where never was heard the blessed tones
Of raindrops pattering on the stones;
And on, still on, like a faded thread,
The desert road still winds ahead.

In the hot, deep and yielding sand,
Her reeling steed at last doth stand.
No stinging lash of man he fears,
Her tender voice, he trembling hears.
Sinking and gasping, to her he turns,
A pleading woe in his dull eye burns,
In the hot sand low lies his head;
O'er him her falling tears are shed,
Forgetful, in her sympathy,
Of human woe and misery;
She kneeling, listens his last breath,
Her faithful servitor 'till death!

Dismayed, her escort by her side
Some word then spoke; and scarce it died
Ere to his horse's back she sprang,
And once again the silence rang
With hoof-beats up the valley drear;
And rising higher, she doth hear:
"Woman! what would you do?" and cried,
"I'd save his life." Then far and wide
Upon the desert's breath was borne:
"Courage! and follow, I will return."

Five miles away, a mountain high,
Rose like a wall against the sky,
And at its base faintly was seen
The blessed sight of forests green.
There too, must crystal waters glide,
And there must men and herds abide.
Five miles o'er burning sands to go,
And in the west, the sun was low;
And wearily her steed did wend
Toward the cruel desert's end.
Nearer, and yes! against the sky
The holy cross lifts to her eye,
In token that below, the town
Nestles against the mountain brown.
Nearer, but slowly as the toll
Of church bells, for the passing soul,
Her tired steed's steps grind in the sand,
And her very life doth seem to stand
Still; while her eyes search far and wide
For the prison town her lord doth hide.
Nearer! its dull gray walls uprise,
Nearer! before her stricken eyes,
Against the wall, erect and bound,
Her heart its king and love hath found!

Staggers her steed to the group of men,
Waiting and watching the sun; and then,
As though she were a crowned queen
Her many thousand troops between,
She looked on them and seemed to wear
The grace and power a queen might bear.
Then she unto their leader spake,
The first, the silence dread to break:
"Senor, before your grace I stand,
And I my lord's release demand."

They looked upon the woman fair
Whose love, had men and desert dared.
And while, for words they vainly sought,
To answer her, who faltered not,
But looking on them, seemed to wear
A halo resting on her hair,
Like a crown's shadow, they but saw
Her beauty, and its spell was law.

Then spake he, and his words did fall
Like benediction over all: .
"I yield him to you, and command
All honor to you from my band."
They loosed his bands, and she had won
His life from death, by set of sun.
O love! what deeds through thee are wrought,
By hearts and hands that falter not.

PARTING.

WHAT brought it back to me?
  I thought that it had fled;
Again I sit with thee
  And watch the twilight red.

Far out upon the deep
  The full moon's light is thrown.
This night thou must not sleep;
  Stay near me, O, my own!

How hard for me to know
  That this must be the last;
That duty's wave must flow
  O'er all the sacred past.

Dear heart, what walls that rise
  Can bar out memory's view,
Or hush the poor heart's sighs
  You'll know are breathed for you?

So fair the moon will rise
  To other eyes than ours,
That weep while bitter sighs
  Stay not the winged hours.

Upon the radiant night,
  From out the thronged halls,
Like requiem to-night,
  The entrancing music falls.

At last the daylight wakes
  With rising shafts of gold,
Each heart in parting breaks,
  And duty's wage is told.

A ROMANCE

*Of the ship "Brooklyn," going from New York
to California*, 1846.

Flags of all lands swing to the breeze,
　　Masts like a forest bare uprise;
Leaving the bay, forth on wild seas
　　The *Brooklyn* goes, 'neath angry skies,

Forth in the winter morning hour,
　　Leaving dear homes and all behind;
Risking the storms, trusting one Power
　　Shall lead them a free land to find.

And friends with tearful eyes may gaze,
　　And strangers pitying turn away;
The ship may sink 'neath cruel waves
　　Or wreck on lonely coast away.

Watching the shore's last line until
　　It fades, in silence, hand in hand,
One, cheerful, young and strong of will,
　　With wife and child, together stand.

And one who walks the city's streets
　　In flush of manhood's morning pride,
Knows not on that lone ship there beats
　　A heart whose fate with his is tied.

And further drifted they apart
　　As gleamed the white sails in the wind;
But there's a charm from heart to heart:
　　The parted each again shall find.

And on past cruel coasts she rides,
  O'er waves that tremble with wreck-wrath;
Past sunny southern slopes she glides,
  A lone ship in a trackless path.

Past gulf and tropic isles they go,
  O'er treacherous reefs of coral red;
Through the equator's stifling glow,
  Warm waves beneath, dull calm o'erhead.

Past where Brazilian plains uplift
  Their idle lengths to mountains high;
Round where Pacific foam-wreaths drift
  To Atlantic blue waves rolling by.

Past where the tawny Spaniards dwell,
  Watching smoke-wreaths 'neath sultry tree;
Towns that in terror trembled, fell,
  As passed the earthquake to the sea.

And gliding past that isthmus dread,
  By blooming, breathing, poisons fanned,
Unconquered yet by freedom's tread;
  And past the buried Aztec's land.

Then wearily, through roughest gales,
  At last within the Golden Gate,
The good ship *Brooklyn* furled her sails
  While war's alarms rang through the State.

Trembling beneath dread Castro's hate,
  Famine by day and guard by night;
When, fainting, sweetly came, though late,
  The boon of peace, like warmth and light.

Bright glowed the fires at many a hearth,
  A ray gleamed from the silent soil,
That glowed like magic o'er the earth,
  And the world's ships thronged to the spoil!

Then rose, in queenly majesty,
  A city young and bright and fair;
One looking from her halls could see
  The world's flags floating harbored there.

And early crowned with beauty, gold—
  Named proud, yet free of heart and hand;
And thrice baptized with flames that rolled
  In ashen robes her structures grand.

Here, 'mid her grandeur, balmy air,
  Down through her flower-gemmed ways went one,
Whose life the silent charm did wear,
  Unconscious how her life should run,

From out these pleasant childhood years,
  To years whose meaning was o'erhung
With mystery, sacrifice and tears,
  With prisoned heart and silent tongue.

Transplanted in a southern land,
  Her life each day unfolded bright,
Through volume, song or landscape grand,
  Fresh charms threw round her life their light.

And here her heart the lesson learned,
  To gain to lose, to shut out trust;
Watched fate slow chill the hopes that burned,
  And lay her idols in the dust.

Along the weary desert road
  Into the mountain-land of snows,
'Mong strangers making her abode,
  Where chosen faith's fair temple rose.

Alone, with heart chilled yet aflame,
  That cried "Wherefore?" to God afar;
When heaviest seemed the life-lot, came
  Up o'er her night its guiding star.

From where God's angel years ago,
  The charmed chain on each one bound;
To here, where she had wandered slow,
  The parted, each again has found.

Bends like an arch the world across,
  The Power that led their feet for years;
Which hath repaid more than her loss,
  Which hath forever hushed her fears.

Dear friend, have you the secret read,
  Whose are the histories herein traced?
Whose feet across the world were led,
  Until they met here face to face?

Ah yes, we know—how can we speak
  The thought swift rising in the heart?
I press your loving hand, your cheek—
  We meet again, no more to part.

A NEW YEAR'S THOUGHT OF BRIGHAM YOUNG.

Dec. 31*st*, 1869.

Down through the music, lights and mirth,
Comes, soft and calm, a thought that turns
The mind aside to that commune
Most sacred, sweet; wherein we see
Life's earnest duties, and feel called
To list God's influence, for His will.

A calm, wherein the mind reads slowly,
Far back down memory's faded page,
Perhaps to sigh—yet, too, may smile ;
For God's forgiveness and His aid,
Forever answer prayer of faith.

To list His influence for His will!
Then, as though angels, pointing, turned,
The heart names softly, Brigham Young.
Do we forget him ?   Thronging cares,
Varying scenes and idle joys
Creep in around us like a screen ;
Hushing and hiding out of sight
Him who stands toiling in the work
God has commanded to be done.
Do we, ungrateful for the guide,
Linger in by-paths by the way ?
Will God forgive us, that we lean
So against his frail threads of life
Our worldly burdens—erring ways ;
That we stand idly, while he calls

Us in the work divine to toil,
And, with indifferent eyes, look past
While he lifts the clouds that hide the way
To the beautiful courts and throne of God?

Again, the music breaking in
Brings to my mind the time, the thought,
Held softly in my mind all day:
To waft a Saint's glad New Year wish
To thee, our Prophet, best loved friend.

A prayer that God's love hold thee safe
From every ill down life's steep way;
That the love and truth of a righteous host
Surround thee strong upon that height
A bitter and jealous world would jar.
That, by power of their obedience,
No law of God through thy lips let fall
But shall be caught up in every heart,
And reign through this happy Zion-land.

That life may freshen in every vein
Through years enduring sweetly on,
'Till silvery halo, softening down
Prime's golden glory round thy brow,
Thou mayest sit in the hush of angels round,
And hear, though far and faint, the fall
Of His footsteps coming upon this earth,
By thy works made ready and waiting Him.
Take the wish of a faithful Saint,
And a glad New Year to Brigham Young.

THOUGHTS WITHIN.

As some poor laborer's sightless babe
Wakes from its pallet on the floor
In fear, to find itself alone,
And gropes the open door to find ;
Reaching anon the empty air
To clutch ; seeking something to grasp
To aid it in its search ; and then,
Wearying in its efforts vain,
It lifts its plaintive, grieving wail ;
Then pauses, listening softly for
Its mother's answering voice ; so I
Kneel down before Thine unseen throne—
So I call to Thee in my prayer
Earnest and deep, yet humble too ;
And listen with that inner ear
Far in the soul's remotest depth.
Not for Thy voice to sweep to earth
Answering to my human cry,
As angels in the old times did,
When men were truly, purely Thine ;
But for an influence, sweet and still,
To lead my groping soul aright.

As though I, clinging to some hand,
Across a torrent spanned but by
A slender tree's decaying trunk,
Looking not to the shore beyond,
Nor turning, though the pine tree shriek
And wave her arms, and writhe in the grasp
Of the dark storm-fiend, strong in his wrath—

Nor on the current swift beneath,
Lest I should, swooning, fall and sink;
But only where my steps should be.
So will I, clinging, follow Thee
Across life's deep, unmindful of
The strife below.

REFLECTION.

THEY come not often, hours like these,
Wherein my life lies bare to me;
Wherein I see, unmasked, unrobed,
Alone, apart from changeful scenes,
Myself.   In panorama pass
Chances misused, or unapplied;
Hours all unsown with deed of good,
Or that still thought which, reaching deep,
Finds, far below, some root of truth;
Wherein, as in a mirror clear,
Myself seems nothing, poor in that
The mind doth yield if tended well.

DEAD.

HUMBLED before such beauty pale,
The holy dignity of death!
We bow the knee, we lowly weep,
We plead with unavailing breath.

Ah, parents! in such solemn hour,
  Our weakness do we learn ;
Nor slight command, nor kind caress,
  Her eye or step again may turn.

To note once more her fragrant breath
  Stir soft her bosom's drapery,
The parent's heart, grown wild with joy,
  Would bless the robes of poverty.
For poorest of the sons of earth,
  In all the many grades that are,
I deem the saddest, loneliest,
  The heart from its beloved afar.

Within that truest of archives,
  The mother's heart ; she aye doth keep
Fair record of the wealth and loss
  Of her beloved, in death asleep.
All that she was! a babe ; the first
  That taught her heart its mother-spell ;
That from her breast looked up, and tried
  The pretty arts she loved so well.

The attempted word, the lightsome step,
  The flush of cheek, the sheen of hair,
The merry laugh, the clear sweet song,
  The grace her every move did wear ;
The promise of what was to be—
  The dawning beauties of her mind,
Where love and duty sweetly blent,
  And wisdom with her joy combined.

Ah! well the parents' hearts might plead
  To watch these buds of hope unfold,
Whose tenderest love their guard should be,
  From every ill that life may hold.

Wherefore, from out such tender care,
   Hath God so far removed thy love?
Unto himself He taketh her—
   Hostage for thy return above.

Where now she is—exalted o'er
   Pain, sorrow, death and power of ill—
She wears such crown we may not wear,
   'Till we have done His sovereign will.
Not blindly, as the world doth mourn,
   We weep the lost from our embrace;
Short is the time when ye shall meet
   Thy best beloved, face to face.

O, carefully live through each day,
   Remembering eyes beloved, that lean
O'er heaven's height, with prayers for thee,
   Faith's golden ladder up between.
And through thy depth of suffering,
   The peace of God will reach to Thee;
And lift thy heart, calmed, to Himself;
   The height and end of love is He.

WHAT GOOD DID IT DO?

"What good did it do?" you asked and smiled,
   As the little one turned away;
Not much, but gladdened the heart of a child
   And made her brief holiday
A brighter spot in her memory
   Than far wiser ones, you or I,
At the crowded counters of costly gifts,
   For our golden coins could buy.

"What good did it do?" you asked, to go
    Spending hours in a darkened room,
When all the wide world outside is aglow
    With sunlight, and flowers in bloom.
O! sweeter the smile on the weary face,
    That the kindness of youth can waken;
When they feel in their age's solitude
    That they are not forsaken.

"What good did it do?" you asked, to spend
    Love's labors and lessons with one,
Stranger and lone, with scarce a friend;
    What good, after all is done?
Before her mirror in loveliness,
    You might have heard the sweet girl's reply:
"Well! the chrysalis of a year ago
    Is changed to a butterfly."

Adown the street at the close of day,
    Came a little herd boy alone;
He was covered o'er with the dust so gray,
    Tired and cold, for winds had blown.
As with downcast head he still onward came,
    Slowly moving his weary feet,
He lifted his eyes, and then flushed with shame,
    At the stranger in the street.

And when she greeted him as she passed,
    Politely, and went on her way,
Little she knew of the spell she cast,
    To be held in his heart alway.
And to himself, as she passed from view,
    "Young lady, you're rich, but not proud;
And if I had been the minister, you
    Couldn't more polite have bowed.

"And I am going from this time forth
  To be good as ever I can;
And of all the women I know on earth,
  I'll marry her when I'm a man."
And he asked her once in after years,
  If she could remember yet
That afternoon, and the words she spoke
  To the tired boy she met.

In a far-off clime, where the air is mild
  And the blossom-time goeth not,
A merchant train out of the desert wild
  An Indian boy had brought,
Who his service gave to come and see
  The wonders wrought in the white man's land,
And to know for himself if the tales were true,
  Of ships, and the waters grand.

And as the traders dallying stayed
  In the lonely seaport town,
The Indian boy, as he idly strayed,
  A resting place and a kind heart found.
"What good will it do to let that boy
  Stay lounging idly about the place?"
And the master turned away with a look
  Of scorn on his handsome face.

A year of travel had come and gone,
  And a lady, with child and guide,
In the desert lone, as the night came on,
  Could her fears no longer hide.
Their horses were weary and faint with thirst,
  The night grew darker and damp,
And the lights ahead—were they of a town,
  Or of an Indian camp?

As trembling they watched the glowing spark—
  "What is it?" in fear the lady shrank,
For a hand caught hers in the awful dark;
  "How do? Don't you know me—Frank?
Don't you remember a year ago
  How you fed me, and let me stay
When the man, who thought I was some one bad,
  Wanted to send me away?

"And do you know you're on the wrong road?
  There's a town, though, a mile below;
I'll bring horses and men to help with the load,
  As fast as my feet can go."
And truer gratitude ne'er was felt,
  Than was hers to the Indian boy;
And to show his own for her kindness, past,
  Was to him the purest joy.

"What good did it do," when you had learned
  The heart, you had thought was so pure,
'Gainst you, who had cherished it so, could be turned;
  Nor temptation's test endure?
Nay, count it no loss; the time will come,
  When the heart, in its own solitude,
Will, repentant, weep o'er thy wounded love,
  And its own ingratitude.

"What good will it do? Ah! never wait
  To count, like a sordid sum,
The worth of a deed, though small or great,
  From a kindly heart just come;
Leave that to Him who alone can know
  What we can but half-way guess:
The power each living creature hath,
  Its kindred heart to bless.

IMMORTELLES.

DEAR love, these immortelles I take,
   Full blown, with all their gloss and sheen,
These buds of palest gold, and make
   A wish for you and and I, between.

So may our hearts together be
   Close bound in an eternal love,
So in our faces shining, the
   Heaven reflected from above.

These flowers' outlines' perfect grace,
   Their waxen lustre pure and clear;
Their star-like beauty, calm and chaste,
   Love's fitting type to me appear.

These flowers, the type of lasting time,
   Deathless gleam up from burial sod;
Pointing like stars unto that clime
   Where tears are not, where dwelleth God.

These flowers! their name a charm enfolds,
   A bride might ask, to bless her way;
Immortal! heaven no blessing holds,
   Higher than immortality.

Immortal spheres in endless turn,
   Immortal lives to spend with Him,
Immortal truths to further learn,
   Immortal beauty ne'er to dim.

Sweet immortelles! your beauty rare,
   Wake in my heart a mute caress;
I bind your name with love's, and wear
   Their deathless beauty in my breast.

DIVIDED HONORS.

It may be true, it oft times seems
　　That I am growing somewhat changed;
That I forget love's early dreams,
　　Grow from those fancies sweet estranged.
Those leisure days, were days when I
　　Had fewer cares to intervene,
And even they might be laid by,
　　Whene'er your presence cheered the scene.

But now another's claims appear,
　　Nor are you envious of her right;
I must divide between you, dear,
　　What was your undivided right.
And please my love, to let no thought
　　Of slight, or loss, create a fear;
The love I give to her is fraught
　　With thought of you, though far or near.

The early dreams live on below,
　　And though unspoken or unlooked;
Are there, as underneath the flow
　　We see the pebbles in the brook.
And, as the stream the long years round,
　　Through sun and storm sings speeding on,
So shall my heart be faithful found,
　　And sing the same while years go on.

And learning better, day by day,
　　Your nature while mine leans to it;
You'll know the semblance, nor will say,
　　"Those early days, do you forget?"

And though my pen not oft indite
Such rhymes I made in idler hours,
Within the heart still glows the light,
All that we had, and more, is ours.

THE COUNTERSIGN.

BELOVED, if oft times you miss
The tender word, the fervent kiss,
Deem not life's poetry has flown,
Or wedded love has graver grown.

Fonder than in the days we met
As lovers, do I view you yet.
Dearer as on in years we go,
Better your worth and truth I know.

No broken faith to wound the heart,
Dividing each lone path apart;
Years passing find us working still
Our walls of faith and love to build—

A temple fair and fit within
For that great Guest to enter in;
Where heart-obedience, faithful ways,
Shall count as anthems to His praise.

Then, though in silence we toil on,
Until the crown and rest are won,
Echoes from thy true heart to mine,
What none else hear, love's countersign.

THE WIFE'S ANSWER.

My wish, responsive to thine own?
I cannot, in a tenderer tone
Than thy dear spirit breathes, express
The thoughts that welling upward press
For utterance; wherein combine
As in a wild-flower wreath, a round
Where grateful love and pride are found.

Love's, duty's, laws I recognize
As right, and all their power prize;
Yielding consent to their decree,
Willing, yes asking it of thee,
The look that shall my course approve,
Or, warning, save me by thy love,
Which with protecting care is thrown
'Round her who trusts thine arm alone.

To know thy worth, to prize as now,
Thy presence, and thy true heart's vow;
To follow thee the world across,
So with thee, counting naught else loss;
My fondest love! my truest friend!
With thee forever to the end;
And ever, true to thee to be,
Is my responsive wish to thee.

TO ANNIE LLEWELLYN.

" For my birthday present, write me a poem."

———————.

AT the remembrance of thy name,
  What kindly, olden memories start!
Here is the gift thou once didst claim
  From out the garden of my heart.

Few are the flowers that grow therein,
  Nor rare, nor bright their clusters shine;
The passer's smile they ne'er might win,
  And Time has faded these I twine.

Here's Hope! How brightly once it bloomed,
  Illuming every day and hour;
And vanquished every cloud of gloom
  That ever hung o'er youth's fair bower.

Here's Love! a flower all have known;
  Has plenty made its value less?
And has it out of fashion grown,
  Which e'er should be the dearest, best?

And here's Forgiveness! blossom pale,
  But little prized and rarely sought,
Amid the shade, adown the vale,
  It blooms with sweetest fragrance fraught.

And here's Remembrance; ivy-like,
  'Round broken hopes and lives it clings,
And deep each tender rootlet strikes,
  And wide its living mantle flings.

But for thy maidenhood's fair time,
　　Too sombre seems the gift I bring :
Like leaves grown sere ere autumn time,
　　Or sadness stealing as we sing.

Yet hope, and may thy dearest dream
　　By love be sheltered and fulfilled ;
And straying hearts will dearer seem,
　　If by forgiveness cherished still.

And, for me, take this rosemary ;
　　If in some oft-read volume pressed,
Its faded leaves will say to thee,
　　Of fair young friends she loved thee best.

TO ROYAL.

AND hast thou come to me, my love,
　　Choosing, o'er every other
Viewed from thine holier home above,
　　Me for thine earthly mother?
Didst thou no dim forebodings feel,
　　Taking on thee the human ;
A helpless, tender child to kneel,
　　Trusting, for guide, a woman?

What wondrous Power directed thee
　　To seek my heart's protection !
Trusting thine unstained soul with me,
　　Thy faith, my benediction !

Ah ! let me take thy hand in mine,
  Thou tender human blossom,
And read in those blue eyes of thine,
  Uplooking from my bosom.

Men may not call me wise or fair,
  Or women care to envy
The humble station that I share,
  Or gifts that fortune sends me ;
But in thy heart, my love, I know,
  Supreme o'er every other,
While life and love together flow,
  Thou wilt love best thy mother.

Then welcome, little stranger dear,
  Unto my heart forever!
And grant that He who sent thee here,
  By death may part us never.
And may I guide these little feet
  By light of holy lessons,
To go with Zion's sons to meet
  His coming, and His blessing.

WOMAN.

THE DAWN OF LOVE.

Thou, who wast yet a child,
  How came it to thy heart?
Becoming, of thy fair life,
  Forevermore a part.

Was it some secret spell,
    Veiled in the depth of a word?
Or was it some charmed tone,
    Thine ear then first had heard?

Was it a whisper, low,
    And gentle as sense of sleep,
That, folding thee softly 'round,
    Led thee to dreamings, deep?

Was it like sudden light,
    Revealing a meaning new:
Tinting thine exquisite cheek
    With still rosier hue?

Touched with a smile, thy lips,
    Lighted anew thine eyes,
Crowned thee and yet veiled thee with
    Silent and sweet surprise.

Was it some noble deed
    On its current swift did bear
Thy soul—or some holy grace
    Led thee as by a prayer?

Erewhile, like crescent pale,
    Behold how thy fair light soon
Grew 'neath this grace of heaven,
    Perfect as the full moon.

Was it like morning mist
    Crowning the sunrise hill?
Or like the mountains firm
    Dost thou behold it still?

No matter:—since thou didst taste
   Of this glowing fountain first,
Thy soul, for its living wine,
   For evermore must thirst.

Then with this light of love,
   Like a lily in thy hand,
Didst thou come within the sphere
   Of womanhood to stand?

Standing within the glow
   Of this new life's fuller light,
Was it with a shrinking heart,
   Or with a calm delight?

Yet never more to thee
   Shall come the same light-winged sleep;
Dreams will pursue thee there,
   Perchance wake thee to weep.

Never again, thy life
   May its youth's sweet faith repeat;
Thou wilt turn with graver eyes,
   Each coming day to meet.

And if unto thy heart,
   Like a whispered prayer doth steal
The mystery of a joy,
   By motherhood revealed;

Thou hast won to thyself
   A jewel that fadeth not;
Yet, with thy rapture, a fear,
   Linked with thy mother-lot.

Yet though above thy head
　　The swift-rising clouds appear,
Thou'rt His daughter, and thy call,
　　Thy Father's soul will hear.

Nearer the grander sphere,
　　Thy journeying daily leads;
Far out from thine earnest soul,
　　The drifting past, recedes.

Thy past—a gentle dream,
　　A folded and hidden page;
Thy present, an earnest life,
　　Seeking an heritage

In still another sphere,
　　Where, through all eternity,
Thy soul shall be satisfied
　　In immortality.

Yet while in faithfulness
　　Thy soul may its mission bear,
And the Father light the way,
　　The thorn-wreath thou must wear.

*　　*　　*　　*　　*　　*　　*

The mother's lot: like Christ to weep,
While loved ones, wearied, sink in sleep;
The mother's lot, like Him to bear
The burden of their wrongs, and wear
A name assailed, if by that cost,
A soul were saved that else were lost.
He died, that souls of men might live;
She, life-long sacrifice doth give.

Too often on her brow doth press
The cruel thorns of thanklessness;
And oft her life its peace hath missed,
Betrayed, too, by a Judas' kiss.
Forget not in thy misery,
The heritage He gave to thee,
To bear, like Him, earth's griefs, and win
A triumph o'er the world within
Thy narrow sphere; and then to share
Reward that greatest love doth bear.

Never recorded to His name—
Stern judgment on thee, weak and shamed;
His charity and wisdom turned
The accuser's blow, and hearts that burned
To wreak their hate and cruelty,
In shame and silence, turned from thee.
And she who came with perfumes sweet,
And, weeping, washed the Savior's feet,
Though sinful, mercy found, and heard
From lips divine, the blest reward—
"Thy sins are all forgiven thee,
And this shall thy memorial be."

For thee, what miracles He wrought!
Thy dead to life again He brought;
The widow's mite He blessed, and she
Lives in His sacred history.
Where'er is told His life divine,
There woman's faith is intertwined.
Never recorded to thy name—
The deed or word, that tongue might claim,
In proof that woman's soul denied

Belief in Him.   Though crucified,
Though cold, inanimate, He lay,
In faith and love no fear could stay
(Mightiest love that ever moved
Hearts in mortality, and proved
Their faith and constancy to Him),
They came while morning yet was dim
In the far east, and weeping brought
Their sacred gifts, and found Him not!

To them who waited through the night
In desolation, for the light,
Nor even yet their Lord could yield
From their existence, He revealed
Fulfillment of His prophecy—
To rise in immortality!
They, who undoubting faith had kept,
O'erjoyed, enraptured, kneeling wept,
With inspiration's eyes to see
The resurrection's mystery!
The first to see the risen Lord,
Thou wert not first to doubt His word;
But first, the wondrous joy to share,
And the glad word ordained to bear.

Though thou hast lost that light of love
    Which made thy path so bright before,
Or though its glow hath died away,
    To shine again for thee no more,
Despair not thou, nor silent turn,
    In wounded pride, to steel thy heart
Against the faithless, when anew
    Thy tender thoughts relenting start.

Too oft demanded in love's name,
　　Such test of thy soul's strength we see,
As greater minds would scorn to bear,
　　And justice ne'er would claim of thee;
'Till wearied, tired, and sore at heart,
　　Thy nature riseth swift to turn
'Gainst all the record of thy hopes,
　　And all their promises to spurn.

Despair not thou, though 'gainst thy soul
　　The wrongs of earth seem to prevail;
Though thou hast yielded all and bowed,
　　Weeping above life's phantoms pale,
Thy heritage to love, and give
　　Thy life's best deeds unto thy kind;
Though that reward, which thou hast earned,
　　Thou ne'er within this life shalt find.

Still to thy standard be thou true,
　　And passing time to thee shall bring
Perfected fruit of all thine aims;
　　And griefs that bowed thee shall take wing.
The ideal within thy soul
　　Is not a fiction of thine own;
Hereafter thou wilt see in full,
　　That which was here but dimly shown.

Thou art not least and last of all
　　In heaven's mighty plan;
Thou too hast place of high degree
　　Beside the soul of man.
Thou wilt not there be counted weak,
　　Though led by love thou art;

In that high court where all is love,
  Such thought will bear no part.
There wilt thou in thy soul redeemed
  The jewel, love, retain;
And wear it as a diadem,
  Not as a master's chain.

Unto this blest and grand estate,
  The gospel lights the way;
Trust thou its guidance, let no doubts
  Thine onward footsteps stay.
O, be thou like the blessed five—
  Thy robes and lamp prepare,
At marriage supper of the Lamb,
  A name and place to share.

FRIENDS.

FRIENDS, dear friends! Awhile ago,
  I thought they were so true, so many!
The wheel of time and change, turned slow
  The summer days to autumn time,
The autumn winds to winter's snow;
  And I in silence and alone,
Half doubted there were left me any,
  Of all that once I used to know.

Yet, as we in forests find,
  When summer's season has departed,
The lofty figure of the pine,
  With dense clad branches reaching out

As shelter to the leafless kind,
   'Gainst warring winds that roughly blow;
So I, friends true and faithful hearted,
   In trial's deepest hour did find.

Friends I thought as true as they,
   I better learned through fortune's changes;
And now I know them, and can say,
   Thanks be to Him for passing storm
That caught the flimsy veil away,
   And left the truer face to view;
Nor mourn the change that did estrange us,
   Sweet summer friends, of a past day!

Over all, a sweet surprise
   Came to my heart its woe to lighten.
Swift as the rainbow to the skies,
   In token that the storm is done,
New friends, like blessed angels rise,
   And I, in silence and alone,
See through the clouds the future brighten,
   Where all was dark before my eyes.

MY BIRTHDAY.

TO MY MOTHER.

DISTANCE and time will only make
   A mother's virtues brighter shine,
And in a daughter's heart awake
   Emotions that but closer twine.

For all the years so richly fraught
　　With worthy store for memory;
Years with all beauty, good o'er wrought,
　　And wisest lessons; can there be.

Time, to repay the tender care,
　　Words, to express the impulse true,
That vainly seeks hereon to bear
　　A daughter's grateful thoughts to you.

All weak and vain my poor essay!
　　Whereby is faintly shown the will,
To thank with love, her, on this day—
　　The first, best friend, and dearest still.

"FOR THE COMING OF THE KING."

*Versification of the story in Frank Leslie's
Illustrated Newspaper.*

SUNLIGHT crowned the grand old Wachtsman,
　　Guardian of the vale below,
And the lesser peaks were flashing
　　With its rays across the snow.

In the warmest nooks, the springtime
　　Seemed awakening, but yet,
Nowhere 'neath the sheltered ledges,
　　Has she found one violet.

Ah, the winter days were dreary!
  And she longed so for the spring,
For his breath blew chill upon them,
  Passing slow with heavy wing.

By the hearth her aged mother
  Murmured 'gainst their misery,
And her wounded brother fretted
  'Gainst their fate in poverty.

And beside, her own beloved
  All has lost through a false friend;
They must longer wait their bridal—
  Ah! where will these troubles end?

Yet from nature all around her,
  When the sun-rays rose and fell,
Came such rapture to her spirit,
  She to him alone could tell.

"Ah," said he, "thou art a poet;
  One whom fortune passes by.
Hadst thou lived in some great city,
  In its schools thy gift to try,

"Thou hadst made thy thoughts of beauty
  Into songs; and they who heard,
Would have sung them." Now, laughed Martel,
  "I shall be like that poor bird

"That we found dead in the snowdrift;
  I shall die, my songs unsung."
But to-day, no happy fancies
  'Round her thoughtful spirit hung.

Looking down the white path winding
   Round the mountain, and away,
Martel sees her own beloved,
   And has something she must say.

"Herman, I have thought of something;
   Thou wilt think it strange, I fear;
And the rest would laugh; I cannot
   Bear it, to be laughed at, dear;"

And he answered, smiling gravely,
   "I will not laugh, never fear."
"Let us then walk on," said Martel,
   "Tis a secret none must hear."

"On the last day before Easter,
   It is said the king will come
To his mother's summer palace,
   And to Munich take her home.

"I shall write him a petition.
   I shall kneel as he goes by
And offer it; I know the way!
   I've thought it over, and shall try.

"I will put it all on paper,
   How the mother's sick, and Hans,
With his wounded hand is helpless;
   And, too, of thy sad mischance.

" I know the king is kind of heart,
   And thou'lt see; yes, thou wilt see!
A good handful of gold pieces
   He will not mind giving me.

"I can scarcely wait for the time,
 I'm so sure that every thing
Will come just right; Oh, how I long
 For the coming of the king."

He had not heart to answer, how
 Common such petitions were;
But looking in her sweet face, thought,
 The king might listen to her.

And weaving plans, with tender love,
 . Through the days that came and went,
Her spirit brightened all their home
 With its secret, sweet content.

The spring had loosened silver streams
 That rippled over mosses green;
And all the town is gay with wreaths,
 Though no flowers yet are seen.

And from stone arches gray and old,
 Words of welcome span the way;
And all the peasants, hastening, throng
 To share in the holiday.

And Martel had not, could not sleep;
 For suspense throbbing in each vein,
And their last meal had been so scant
 She an earlier meal has feigned.

Ah, poor Martel, she was living
 On the wine of hope, to-day;
And it seemed to have reached her brain
 And stolen all her calm away.

"Such a day! mother, the sunshine
   Is dancing, and so could I."
"Thou'rt so light headed," grumbled she,
   "There's no other reason why."

"That is my secret"—then she laughed—
   "A little bird told it to me."
"I wish I had him broiled," cried Hans;
   And then dressed, the king to see,

Though he had vowed he hated kings,
   And ne'er wished to see one more;
The mother, too, went with a friend,
   All their woes recounting o'er.

Around her glossy yellow braids,
   Then her silken scarf she tied;
And silver arrow in her hair,
   Fastened with a modest pride.

And if the king not gracious proves,
   That too, before the night must go!
Ah no! the good God would not let
   Her prayers all fail her so.

"Martel, thou art transfigured!" cried
   Her lover, "one might well believe
Thy petition had been offered,
   And thou hadst its boon received."

Said she, with sweet solemnity,
   "Ah, I have been offering
A petition, and I know
   'Tis accepted, by that King."

Her heart beat faster as she looked
　　At the paper she had planned;
And the Easter lily on it,
　　Held within her trembling hand.

There were cries, the king was coming,
　　And they hurried down the street,
Where the queer old houses crowding,
　　Left no space for gardens sweet.

A shout! the band plays! now's the time—
　　"Martel, shall I go with thee?"
"Oh, no; where are Hans and mother?
　　Stay and wish God speed for me."

She steps forward, and up-holding
　　The petition in her hand,
And the lily white upon it,
　　Kneels before them in the sand.

Ah! the horses start affrighted;
　　Just one moment the sweet sound
Of the music is around her,
　　And the blue sky smiling down;

And the next, a horror crushes,
　　Blackness drops before her eyes,
And above the burst of music
　　Cries of agony arise.

Did she cry, or was it Herman,
　　As he saw his little love,
And sprang forward and has caught her
　　From the hoofs that rear above?

Some one picks the broken lily,
  And the paper from the sand,
And reading on it, "For the King,"
  It is laid in his own hand."

Martel opens eyes that wonder,
  How strange all the faces are!
Only one, her Herman's, clearer—
  She is drifting from them far.

And she cries, "Oh hold me, keep me!
  I am waiting for the King."
Little Martel, thou shalt meet him,
  Thou shalt soon behold thy King.

By her side the poor old mother,
  And the brother, weeping, kneel;
And she sees them, smiling faintly,
  She no sense of pain can feel.

"See! she cries! the Easter lilies!
  Herman come pick them with me.
The king has given me all this gold.
  Ah! how happy we shall be!

"And the king read her petition,"
  Martel, dear, couldst thou not wait?
For the dear one's tears are falling
  "On the royal gift, "too late."

THE ROMANCE OF LEONARDO DA VINCI.*

SWIFT passing down the silent street,
  Beneath a wall with vines o'erhung,
He paused before a gateway dark,
  And as he waited, softly sung.
Then gently swung the gate ajar,
  And where the boughs dense shadows cast,
Moved a shadow among shadows
  He, laughing, caught at, as it passed.
"Ah! little one, I have you safe."
  "Why do you tremble so, my dove?
Rest tranquil, child, and tell me true,
  Are you not glad to see me, love?"

"Ah, so glad! so heavenly glad,
  But I could not rest for fear
That you would not come, and ventured
  To look if you were surely here."
He drew her to a seat beside him,
  And 'round her form so fair and slight,
He folded close his heavy cloak,
  To shield her from the air of night.

"Cara, I have much to tell you,
  And little time ere I must go;"
He bent his face to kiss her own;
  She started—"Don't, Signor; you know
Our proverb," and repeated soft,
  "A woman kissed, is one disgraced."

*—Versified from the "Romance of the Village of Vinci," by Mrs.
Enoch Root, in the *Western Magazine.*

"But you are not a woman," said
  He, looking in her lovely face;
"You are my little one, my child;"
  And added in a fonder tone,
You are mine only, my own love,
  And truly I may kiss my own."
"Now, dearest, while I speak not time
  Is passing. Ah, how short it seems
Since first I saw you, kneeling, fair
  As any saint of holiest dreams.
And when on passing out you looked
  On me, dear child, I kept that look,
And one day I shall show the world
  The face that to my heart I took:
The only woman that I love.
  When I return, beloved, then—"
"Are you going to leave Florence?
  Maestro, I shall see you—when?"

"I am going to leave Florence;
  Listen, and I will tell you why.
I, who was famed ere he was born,
  To listen to his praise! and I
To take a place second to him,
  This Buonarrotti! I, who can
Do what any other one may,
  No matter who may be the man!
No, no, dear child, I go to France."
  "To France! Ah, Dio!" and she pressed
Her hands upon her stricken heart,
  As though to crush its keen distress.

"'Tis only for a little while,
  My darling; nay, do not grieve so;

I've seen the king at Pavia,
　Now he desires me, and I go.
When I have taught these Florentines
　I can in any country do
Whate'er I will, I will return;
　I will return, dear child, to you.
And then, will you be ready to
　Become my wife?" "His wife," said she
Looking steadfastly in his eyes,
　Like one bewildered with the joy
　Revealed in this supreme surprise.
Looking into her earnest face,
　He said, "You do not know aright
Even my name; but I will give
　It to you ere I go to-night.
And when I come for you, no one
　Will then deny me." Though she heard
His words of love and hope, a shade
　Of woe seemed veiling every word.

"But you will not stay long! Oh, love,
　I fear so much, you're leaving me
For a long journey. Can I live?
　I'm only happy when I see
You often; I am not a rose,
　Only a field flower blooming on
While you my sun shine on me; I
　Shall fade and die when you are gone."

"My child, then do you love me so?"
　"How can you ask? Can you not see
I cannot bear it? O, my love,
　I die, now you are leaving me."

He drew her closer to his side;
   "I do believe and trust in you,
My jewel; you will be repaid
   For all the waiting long and true.
Now I must go; nay, grieve not so,
   But keep a brave heart for my sake,
And here, my darling, is the name
   That you one day ere long will take.
But now regard it not, for I
   Must have your every thought, my love.
Ah, could I but take you with me!
   Come to my heart, cling close, my dove.

"Back, love, out of the moonlight, for
   I cannot see your tears, they make
A woman of me." Then he knelt,
   A last and sad farewell to take.
"Farewell, my life!" Gently he placed
   Her on the garden seat and passed
Out through the gate. Silent she stood,
   All desolate, and then at last
Thought of the paper. Lifting it,
   In the clear moonlight read the name,
Then raised it to her lips, and in
   An ecstacy of tears exclaimed:
      "Maestro! oh, Maestro!
      I wait for thee forever."

The days and months and years passed on,
   And while she waited, now and then
Came like an echo from the world,
   His fame among earth's greatest men.
Ah, was it not enough! how long
   Ere he would come? Did he forget?

And what is fame, weighed against love
   Through all life's changes faithful yet?

As down through life she silent passed,
   Men loved, and stayed her just to speak;
But on her heart their words fell dull,
   Nor e'en called to her pallid cheek
The flush replying to love's tone.
   She heard, and answered and went on,
Nor feared the change that years might bring
   To her, alone, of age, friends gone.
Brighter than youth, nearer than friends,
   Her heart still held, dearer than these,
In its own hidings, that commune
   The sweetest, truest memories.

O, love! if living, speak to me.
   Though e'er so far, still I shall know;
Speak in the nightfall; it will come,
   Though floating soft and faint and slow.

I wander through these narrow streets,
   These streets where once your feet.have been;
My heart still o'er and o'er repeats
   The parting vow you made me then.
How strange it seems that I am here,
   Here where you waited for so long,
I almost seem to feel you near,
   To feel your presence in the throng.

I watch the sunset's flame die out,
   The twilight fades, the day is dead;
Alone I sit, I hear your voice
   And dream o'er all your lips have said.

The moonlight pale falls on the hills
    That stand in silent witness there;
So comes the white pain in my face,
    The snow-cold mantle of despair.

The years pass on, no tidings come,
    So stirless, voiceless lies my past,
I almost deem my pain o'ercome—
    Through heaven's pity soothed at last,
Till I might deem e'en hope were dead;
    Some passing face awakes it all—
I wake to watch though hope has fled,
    And through hushed breath the chill tears fall.

Who calleth life's first loving weak—
    A dream that after years may fade?
It liveth in the pallid cheek
    And in the sorrowing eyes' deep shade—
Unseen through years that come and go,
    It bends communing as they pass;
'Till life's flush fading into snow,
    Speaks to the heart, 'tis o'er at last.

Beloved, last night I dreamed you came—
    Came with fond greeting and caress;
And my poor heart of chill and flame,
    Sobbed out upon your faithful breast,
All woe these years had garnered in;
    'Till in your presence, as of old,
Your majesty and grace wherein
    All right of rightful love was told,

My heart found comfort, and forgot
    All save that hour's separate spell;

And joy and rest bore but one thought:
  Your presence and its peace, that fell,
Enfolding sweetly 'round my heart,
  A hush, a calm, wherein at last,
Amid its bliss, I paused to start—
  And waken from a dream—and past.

*   *   *   *   *   *   *

And when they brought her forth with them
  To mingle in the dance and song,
Like one alone, and half a-dream,
  She strayed amid the festal throng.

And thus her life endured,
  Which else had loosed its hold—
But for the thought he yet might come,
  And ne'er the truth be told,
Of her heart's constancy to him
  Which all love's tests endured.

*   *   *   *   *   *   *

Where hast thou gone, dear friend?
  I missed thee when I came;
Music and light and joy were there,
  Thou didst not call my name;
A subtle something wrapped me 'round,
  And joy and zest had end.

And which way didst thou pass
  From out our happy throng,
That we should never meet again
  Through all life's journey long,
Whose guidance o'er my early path
  Must light it to the last?

Over those vanished days,
  That dream-like now appear,
An influence thy presence wrought,
  That even yet is near,
As when I strove to shape my life,
  As thou wouldst wish or praise.

What, though the years are gone,
  And I am turning gray?
Part of my life stopped, missing thee,
  And waiteth there to-day
Where thou didst charge me wait for thee,
  While passing time went on.

When thou wert by my side,
  Each feeble power of mine,
Inspired by thy influence,
  With fairer light did shine ;
And harmonies swept through the whole,
  And faltering discords died.

Often thou seemest near.
  I pause and stay my breath—
Where art thou? In this prison life,
  Or from that side of death,
Return thy faithful thoughts to me
 . To prove I still am dear?

By token of that truth—
  Our immortality—
(And that life's cherished, purest joys,
  Eternal too shall be ;)
I know that there will be unveiled,
  The mystery of our youth.

Therefore, I still can wait,
  Striving, through passing years,
To live a life so worthy thee,
  That, when thy soul appears,
Thou'lt know my heart its vow hath kept,
  Though waiting long and late.

   *   *   *   *   *   *   *

In a room where shadows hovered
  Over pictures, statues, curtains,
Where each object lost its outlines
  In the wav'ring light uncertain,

Lay a dying man—one weary
  Of earth's praises—with one only,
A poor student, loving, faithful,
  Watching by this bedside lonely.

Wistfully the sad eyes wandered,
  And, wearily, from side to side,
He turned his head, as though to seek
  The peace that fleeting time denied.

"Alas, dear friend, it is no use,
  I am fast leaving you, and there
Is no one else in all the world
  For whom I have a love or care.

"There was one, but after I came
  To France, they came and brought me word
That she had married. I did wrong
  In then believing what I heard.

"I should have sought the truth myself,
    For as the mists of life give way,
All things look different, and she
    Seemed very good and pure alway.

"If she indeed be yet alive,
    Then she will hear that I am gone;
And where I go I shall see her,
    For I have loved no other one,

And she will know."   And softly then
    He called her name, as she were there.
"Maestro, what is there to do?
    Is there a message I could bear?"

"In vain, dear friend, I am too weak,
    No, no, alas it is too laté,
I was too ready to believe
    The story; why did I not wait?"

He turned his head and earnestly
    Looked on a portrait small and rare,
A tender face with wondrous eyes
    And waving, glossy, raven hair.

The student, seeking to divert
    Him from sad thoughts, spoke of his fame,
How in all countries, his success
    Had crowned with highest praise his name.

Then passed across the sick man's face
    A smile of mingled pride and scorn.
"I knew my name would stand the first,
    I had won fame ere he was born.

"I have not cringed to pope or king!
  Oh fame, what have I given for you?
My Italy, and my own love—
  My darling, I know you were true."

Softly the door swung open then,
  And unannounced within the room,
A stately gentleman drew near
  And stood within the deep'ning gloom.

The dying man essayed to raise
  His head in reverence to his guest,
But was too weak. "Nay, do not move,"
  Exclaimed his visitor, distressed;

"I heard that you were ill, and would
  Come and see for myself how you
Were faring." An answering smile
  Lighted the artist's face anew:

"Your majesty has given the
  Greatest happiness possible;
Even as the same gen'rous hand
  Has made my last days beautiful."

Then the king, bending o'er his couch,
  Answered, "Nay, do not speak of thanks;
The greatest artist of all time,
  I've made my friend, and kept in France."

He reached as though to clasp a hand;
  And the king, thrilled with swift alarms,
Before the youth could reach his side,
  Raised the Maestro in his arms.

A change, a calm and grandeur, o'er
   The features of the dying lay;
And, resting in his sovereign's arms,
   The artist's soul had passed away.

        *   *   *   *   *

"So strange," said the two old women—
   "She would not marry Vincencio,
Neither enter a convent; you
   Heard how her spirit, years ago

"Appeared before them at their wine?"
   "What story? when? I did not know."
"Oh, long ago! ten years or more;
   They were all in the Albergo,

"And the Master who used to come
   To our village paid for the wine.
So you see how they remember--
   'Twas when he came here the last time.

"As I said, they were all drinking,
   When, as plain as you now see me,
Agatina went past the door,
   So plain, there no mistake could be.

"Not a step did they hear, as one
   Would hear a mortal woman; they
Ran to the door: no one was there—
   Gone like a spirit—so they say.

"And the next morning she was pale,
   She had that far, lost-look, and changed,
She has had ever since. Surely,
   'Twas warning of some trouble strange.

"Here goes Vincencio, just returned
From Florence.   Tell us friend, what word
Of news, if you have any brought?"
"Sad news have I in Florence heard;

"The great Maestro who was born
Here in our town, has died, they say,
In France, in the arms of the king."
"Ah, well! how grand to die that way!"

"Ah, Madre, here goes the shadow."
"Stay, Agatina, have you heard
The sad news?   Whither do you go?"
"I go to Church; but what sad word

"Is't you would tell me?"   "Ah, poor child,
'Tis not sad news for us, for he
Was far above us; but the great
Maestro whose home used to be

"Here in our town, has died in France,
Died in the king's arms, too, they say;
Was that not grand?"   "Dead? ah, Dio!"
She looked on them, then turned away

And slowly walked towards the church,
And they in wonder shook their heads;
"Ah, the poor child, she certainly
Has become foolish;" each one said.

And steadily she still went on—
"Dead," murmured she, "then all is o'er;
I did wait, dear Maestro, I
Did trust, but he came back no more."

She entered the dim church and knelt
　Before the virgin and the Child ;
And gazed up into the still face
　That on the kneeling figure smiled.

The sweet face that he kissed farewell,
　Was sadly changed, was ghastly now ;
The dark eyes burned with feverish light,
　The hair was gray about her brow.

She clapsed her thin transparent hands
　And looked up to the holy face,
As though the mystery of her life
　Might in its tranquil smile be traced.

"Thou knowest I was true," she moaned,
　"And now he knows." The eyes above
Looked down in hers, and then she thought
　The lips moved with a pitying love.

"He said when he returned that this
　Would be my name. Why did he not
Come for me? shall I go to him?"
　She looked up in the face and thought
The mother smiled. She bowed her head,
　"Yes, I shall go to him," she said.

The peasants entered the dim church,
　Knelt, and went one by one away ;
The guardian looking at her, thought,
　"Poor child, she says many prayers to-day."

At last the priest, passing inside
    The railing where the figure knelt,
Stretching his hand in blessing forth,
    He knew not why a shudder felt;

And touching her, beneath his hand
    The silent, kneeling figure swayed!
He caught, and on the pavement cold,
    Gently the lifeless form he laid.

The weary face was rested now;
    The eyes no longer watched for one
Who came not. And the loving heart
    The prayer to go to him had won.

From wasted fingers they drew forth
    The crumpled paper as to claim
The secret, and in wonder read!
    Leonardo da Vinci's name.

THE PAINTER AND THE PLEDGE.

ABOVE his work the artist leaned,
    His eager hand was weak,
The shadows deepened in his eyes,
    And paler grew his cheek.
For want, within the artist's home,
    Its chill and gloom had cast;
The fire had died upon his hearth,
    While driving snows swept past.

His lips were dry and faint for food,
　And still, while hours went on,
He wrought, to stay and hold the prize
　His soul from heaven had won.
But o'er its beauty, through his heart,
　A tide of anguish swept;
His trembling hand let fall its work;
　The artist bowed and wept.

Yet, in the darkened sky above,
　Clouds rifted, and there stole
A spark of light—a thought of hope
　' To cheer the artist's soul.
And while he gazed upon its beam,
　Wider its light was spread,
And faith and hope in blessing brought
　Their peace upon his head.

He stood before a man of wealth,
　His plea the rich man weighed;
"What pledge hast thou to leave with me,
　If I should give thee aid?
If I should for thy present need
　Lend thee my shining gold,
Wilt thou thy picture pledge to me,
　When finished, 'till 'tis sold?"

The artist bowed his head in thought:
　What price, for palty sum!
And blushed that from his brother-man
　Such stinted deed should come;
Yet thought, "Shall I for selfish pride,
　Hide from the world the prize
My soul has found, that I alone
　May lift from where it lies?

I pledge it to thee if thou'lt grant
   This deed in turn to me :
That it shall hang in public place
   Where men shall pass and see ;
And if to win it for its worth,
   Some gen'rous hand shall come,
Thou wilt restore my work to me,
   Receiving back thy sum.

"I pledge it to thee, merchant prince—
   The task God gave my soul
Is not for mine own joy alone ;
   My hand may not withhold
Its service in the work He set.
   Birds that He made for song,
Refuse not ; and then why should man
   His gift, God-given, wrong ?"

The artist wrought the task he loved,
   But through day after day
The pledge upon his work, his word,
   Like chains upon him lay.
'Till every touch of joy therein
   Seemed softened and subdued,
As lilies purest seem to grow
   In shadows of the wood.

'Twas finished.   Idly first they paused,
   The stranger's work to view,
Then passed its fame from lip to lip ;
   And daily still they drew
In silent groups that, wondering,
   In its still beauty traced
Some sign to every human heart,
   Whate'er in life its place.

Looking upon it, Virtue seemed
    Lovelier than before,
And hearts, that followed Evil's smile,
    Listened its call no more;
And Mammon's worshipers were turned
    To count their wealth as dross,
And Sacrifice, before its spell
    Gave all nor called it loss.

"Let this be mine," the merchant said,
    "Mine is the earliest claim;
I will not grudge thee any price
    In gold, that thou may'st name."
"Nay, 'tis too late," the artist spake,
    "'Twas pledged thee until sold.
Another hand hath won the prize,
    And I have brought thy gold."

JACK FROST AND THE MORNING-GLORIES.

All the summer long she played,
    Where, trained up on slender lines,
A sweet summer-house was made
    Of the morning-glory vines.

When the early morning broke
    The soft hush of gentle night,
At the first bird-call she woke
    With a welcome for the light.

And with happy haste she sought
　Her loved bower with joy, to view
The miracle that night had wrought—
　Wealth of flowers of every hue.

While she wondered, 'round her came
　Humming birds with gauzy wing,
Fearing not; and robins, too,
　Just above her perched to sing.

And, when high, the sun threw down
　Shadows that a pattern made,
Like a carpet on the ground,
　Where the little lady played.

And so fair the summer hours
　Passed, like an unbroken dream,
That the life this pet of ours
　Lived, like fairy story seemed.

But, one morning, when we woke,
　Fall had come, the air was cold;
And her bower—at one stroke,
　Bloom and leaf were brown and old.

Not a butterfly in sight,
　Not a single humming bird;
Wilted, every blossom bright—
　What would she say when she heard?

Turning, she was at my side:
　She had seen the picture drear;
To speak steadily she tried—
　"'Tis Jack Frost who has been here."

"Yes, my child, he comes and goes
    When and wheresoe'er he will;
Free as rudest wind that blows,
    None can check or thwart his will."

"No," she said, "there is a place
    Where his footsteps dare not roam."
Answering me, with pensive grace:
    "In my heavenly Father's home."

COMPARISON.

My children played in happy health,
    My home was small and neat;
Above the door, a branching vine
    Shed wealth of fragrance sweet.
I closed the gate and looked once more,
    Fair order and content
Prevailed o'er all; and, satisfied,
    On duty's call I went.

Around, within, the rich man's home,
    By bounteous wealth supplied,
Treasures of beauty and of worth
    Appeared on every side.
And while I looked, comparison
    A shade regretful lent;
My thoughts turned from my little home
    In blush and discontent.

Then from the rich man's home I turned,
  And near a dusty road,
I found the object of my search
  In ruined, lone abode.
Within were want and gloom and grief;
  Too late I came—for death
Had hushed the moan for want and food,
  And stilled the sufferer's breath.

My children ran to greet me home,
  Ah, sweet seemed life and health!
They asked a kiss, and shamed my heart
  That had wished greater wealth.
And when they slept, I went to Him—
  "Blest be Thy will," I said;
"Thou hast not made me rich in gold,
  Nor mourner o'er the dead."

AT MY WINDOW.

"Thou art so near, and yet so far,"
  Availing naught while hoping all;
So near, that through my curtains' folds,
  Thy tapers' rays like moonlight fall.

So near, I hear thy sweet voice pour
  Some air of thy far native land;
So far, we meet, we greet and pass—
  A smile, a look, a touch of hand.

7*

So near, that falling into sleep,
    My face turns towards thy taper's beam ;
So far, that days may come and go,
    Without exchange of words we dream.

So near, the time when I must go,
    To come again, perhaps no more,
So far from thee ; unfinished too
    The dreams of hope framed o'er and o'er.

Yet shall I bear away with me
    A joy that I have known thy face,
An arch of beauty o'er my path,
    Like moonlight o'er some lonely waste.

----•-•----

HOW SHALL I KNOW?

How shall I know what I wish to know?
    How shall my heart find rest?
Shall the sweet thoughts that like soul-lights glow,
Tremble as now, and stronger grow,
    Or quiver and tremble and sink to rest,
Quenched by the tears that sadly flow?

Shall the sweet hope that has long been mine,
    Tremble and fade away?
Or will it brighter and brighter shine,
Lighting my way with a light divine—
    A hope that is pure as the beam of day,
And richer than treasures of sea or mine?

And when at life's sunset I bend my knee,
  With gray hairs crowning my brow,
As bright will the future still seem to be,,
Still will the past be as dear to me,
  Still will the thought of my heart's first vow,
Lead me, Father, to heaven and Thee?

VIOLETS AND APPLE BLOSSOMS.

AFFIANCED.

DREAMING of you I bind these buds,
Weaving down in my heart a hope,
That I may be with you and be yours
When these shall bloom again.
When these shall bloom again, dear love!
Only a year, and yet how long
Ere their lovely blush again shall burn
On the cheek of spring; ere their lovely blue,
The blue of your eyes, shall upward look
From the bank of the river that ripples on,
Hastening on to the mighty sea.

Dreaming of you through all the hours,
  Weaving hopes for you, love, by day;
Weaving prayers for you, love, by night:
  Heaven be kind to you, dear, alway.

They knew not my heart—a guarded hall,
Ever closed, and you hold the key.
Keep it forever! that none but you
May tread or speak in its sacred hush;

That only your eyes may see on its walls
The glowing pictures of love and thought ;
That only your ear may hear the strains
Ever breathing from love's sweet harp.

————◆●◆————

ADELAIDE-IE.

————

THE sunset hues had died away,
  The twilight's gentle hour had passed,
· And overhead the deep'ning shades
  Of the still night were gath'ring fast.

I laid my pen aside, and leaned
  Back in my chair; when lo! a spark
Of light strayed through my window pane,
  Directly to me, through the dark.

It wavered o'er my weary hands,
  Across my paper travelled on ;
It climbed shelf after shelf of books,
  Just touched the ceiling, and was gone.

And though I roused from dreamy mood,
  I had no thought of wond'ring fear,
For, with the sound of children's feet,
  I heard a voice call sweet and clear.

Adown the hillside path they went,
　Swinging a lantern through the dark,
To bring the little sister home;
　This was the secret of the spark.

They never called her real name,
　For the winsome little lady
Had chosen one that pleased herself,
　And that name was, Adelaide-ie.

Somehow, it pleased and freshened me,
　And after light and voice were gone,
·My spirit saw in this a thread
　To hang a pleasant fancy on.

Has not our Father love like this,
　Though late and far from him we roam,
To send some angel with a light,
　Who'll call and bring the dear one home?

COMING HOME.

THE days creep ling'ring onward
　While I count them one by one,
And gladly I look backward
　O'er the months of waiting done.

The spring calmed down its beating
　To the calmer pulse of June;
Now the autumn days are fleeting,
　And the willows sigh the tune

They will sing in louder measure,
    When the winter days are here,
To crown with crystal treasure
    The King-Day of the new year.

Come and pass, O winter hours!
    Bid the happy spring return,
With her blushing cheek and flowers;
    Come, O summer, blush and burn;

Hush the chill wind on your breast,
    Hush the moaning of the sea,
Rock the cradled deep to rest,
    Light his way, O stars, to me!

Coming home! my heart keeps singing
    These sweet words through all the day;
Coming home, and harvest bringing
    From his mission far away.

THY CHARITY.

THY charity, oh! let it be
Like hidden seed that none may see.
Enough that thou hast placed it there,
And heaven will guard it in its care;
And from the heart where it was sown,
Sweet praise will make thy kindness known.

Thy charity may wound, not bless,
If added to a heart's distress
That charity should seek to hide;
Thy hand should tear the veil aside;
And keener far this grief may be
Than e'en the sting of poverty.

Thy charity! It is not so!
It is a stealthy, cruel blow—
A Judas kiss, if thou hast named
The deed that human need hath claimed.
Thy heart is proved, thy love is weighed,
And wounded pride the debt has paid.

Gold pays the debt of gold; no more.
Gold cannot unto thee restore
The implicit faith to thee was given,
If by rude touch it once is riven.
Thy words have pierced, thy gifts were vain—
"The wound may heal, the scars remain."

DESPAIR.

BREATHE not to me the idle word,
  Hope! for some fairer day will shine;
Let not by its sweet tone be stirred
  This drooping, spirit sad, of mine.

With broken, bleeding wing she sleeps
  In sunless niche where echoes die;
The bitter tear no more she weeps,
  Pours forth no more the burning sigh.

For, she hath, weary, yielded all—
    Youth, hope, companionship and mirth;
Turned the deaf ear to pleasure's call,
    And asks no more from lips of earth.

Aye! asks no more, to be denied
    The crumbs from plenteous hands let fall;
While worldlings reveled, in her died
    Her life's vain courage, 'gainst it all.

So speak not ye the charmed sound,
    Lest this poor heart should wake again;
Bring not to light, and touch, the wound
    Beneath the stifling feels no pain.

So, let it sleep, nor breathe the word
    Might wake a sorrow turned to scorn,
And o'er its freshened pang be heard
    The break, of a life from earth upborne.

PRESENTIMENT OF COMING ILL.

My heart is full of passion wild,
    My brain is awake, and will not rest;
Here let me lie, like a little child
    That cries out its woes on its mother's breast.
With the rushes that, towering, hide out all,
    The street and the house, from my nervous eyes,
With the soothing cool from the waterfall,
    And the trees, that like giant guardsmen rise;

With the tangled grass for my pillow and bed,
  And the silence, to calm this fevered head—
Here let me lie, like a little child
  That cries out its woe on its mother's breast.

The daisies nod their heads in dreams,
  The violets bow with saintly grace;
Wilder rócks my heart with its restless dreams,
  Their purity mocks the strife in my face;
This silence is deeper and wilder than all!
  Let me sing, let me sing! 'till echoes wake
The dark pine-guards on the mountain wall.
  Let me sing! this silence my heart will break!
O voice! from my soul's wild, sorrow-tossed sea,
  You float clear and high, like a thing set free;
Wilder rocks my heart with its restless dreams—
  Your purity mocks the strife in my face.

Deeper the soul-pain sinks and burns,
  My hands are fettered, my eyes are blind;
Hopeless, my spirit wearily turns,
  Seeking the aid she knows not where to find.
What is it falleth so close and thick,
  Like a muffled terror, about my heart?
I hold the rein on my breathings quick,
  But my brain rides wild, my pulses start;
Viewless, silent, vague, on the empty air,
  Of what, would I speak, did I breathe a prayer?
Hopeless, my spirit wearily turns,
  Seeking the aid, she knows not where to find.

Floateth afar, the strange presence, then fast,
  Close to my side, when my soul thought release;
O bend to me! pity, stand close till it pass—
  Close, close, though I tremble, sweet spirit of peace.

For this ill riseth fast, like the up-creeping wave,
　Where the fisher-girl peers through the dark for her way;
And the terror is wild as the waters that rave,
　And the prayer-cry thrills broken in echoes away.

＊　　＊　　＊　　＊　　＊　　＊　　＊

Through a rift in the sky, breaks a ray smiling warm,
There's a prayer far away, breaks the spell of the storm.
Rising soft like a psalm, mem'ry brings me release—
Cling close lest I lose thee, sweet spirit of peace.

FAIRY FINGERS.

FAIRY fingers! whose are they,
　That have brought, the while we slept,
Tropic leaves and lovely spray
　Where no garden e'er was kept;
Fastening in groupings rare,
　Wreaths impearled and jeweled bright,
Delicate beyond compare,
　Fairest in the clearest light ?

Strange ! yet none could ever catch
　Sight of them at work or play.
Though from sleep an hour we snatch,
　They evade us and away.
Who has ever caught a glimpse
　Of the dainty, busy things?
Are they merry, prankish imps?
　Are they fays with filmy wings?

When I closed the door last night,
   Not a sign of this was here,
It was still, the moon shone bright,
   And the sky was very clear.
But this morning, every weed
   Wore a veil of fairest lace,
Silver fringe and pearly bead,
   With the utmost, native grace.

And e'en every rustic post,
   (Matters not how rude they are,)
A new ermine cap can boast,
   . Gemmed with many a shining star.
Long I dwelt in summer land,
   Yet I never saw such sight—
Bush and tree on every hand
   Uniformed in purest white.

In my window—such design,
   Ne'er has mortal artist drawn!
Come and make the pattern thine,
   For thy lace work, ere 'tis gone.
With what skill, and by what means,
   Were these dainty things brought forth
O'er the space that intervenes
   From the far wilds of the North?

Ah, how beautiful! the sun
   Rises, and his slanting beams
Touch the crystals, and each one
   With the rainbow's glory gleams.
Wondrous workers, ere I go
   Tell my spirit rapture lost,
Who have wrought this? Whisper low!
   And they answered, "'Tis the frost."

L I F E .

THE young man dreams, with impatient heart,
  Of the world so fair and wide,
And longs to journey the unknown path,
  With his own free will for guide.
He dreads no storm, and he has no fear,
  For his heart is young and strong ;
His soul is pure and its armor on,
  For the warfare 'gainst all wrong.

And over the bygone centuries
  Rise the shining heights of Fame,
And his will is strong to write thereon,
  With some noble deed, his name.
His dreams are all of the coming time,
  And the past is little prized :
A flower dropped, that memory yet
  Will lift up from where it lies.

The old man rests in his easy chair,
  The journey of life is done ;
And he turns to home as the truest joy
  That his life's long search has won.
He dreads the contest of right and wrong,
  For his heart has weaker grown ;
And who, in the tumult, heeds the voice
  Of one obscure and unknown ?

His dreams are all of the precious past,
  And he loves, the best of all,
To recall the life in the dear old home,
  Ere he heard the great world's call.

Brighter to him than fame's shining heights,
  The gold of his grandchild's hair ;
She has pinned on his breast, not a badge,
  But a rose, for him to wear.

But the little child, at its happy play,
  For the past nor the future sighs,
And the passing present to her yields,
  In every hour, a prize.
The strength of youth may fail in the strife,
  Wisdom by wrong be beguiled ;
Worthy the kingdom of heaven alway,
  The soul of a little child.

ART THOU SINCERE?

ART thou sincere, dear friend ?
  Thou dost perplex me so ;
I'd give, ah, what would I not give,
  The honest truth to know.

I know that thou art loved,
  I know that thou art wise ;
Thy winning smile, thy voice's tone,
  Wherein such meaning lies,

Charm all my being through
  With so refined delight,
My soul revives beneath the spell,
  As birds wake with the light.

Hours, I have known with thee,
　Held sense of beauty, bliss;
That in all friendships heretofore,
　My spirit's search had missed.

I would not check thy smile,
　I would not cause a shade
Of trouble to o'ercloud those eyes,
　For all the gold e'er weighed.

When thou dost greet me with
　A smile, my heart is light,
And, singing, goes upon its way;
　And life seems good and bright.

And yet, sometimes, I miss
　Thy welcome; then how strange!
My heart shrinks from thee, wondering
　Whate'er hath wrought the change.

And so, oft times, will come
　The thought, and wake a fear;
Which is the truth: thy seeming love,
　Or art thou insincere?

Away! dark shade of doubt;
　Thou art unworthy her;
Shall I, contrasted with her smile,
　Thine evil frown prefer?

And yet—unanswered yet,
　O friend! so prized, so dear;
I pray thee, whatsoe'er the truth,
　Be thou to me sincere.

THE LILAC TREES.

MANY a towering, lordly tree
　The dear old farm could boast;
The ancient, spreading sycamores,
　My father prized the most.

We children, linking hands, would try
　How many it would take,
Of us, with arms around the trunk,
　A measurement to make.

Many a kind from other climes,
　With pride and care were sought;
The stately and the beautiful,
　To grace our home were brought.

Yet, though these far-fetched treasures won
　Praises of many a guest,
Somehow, down in my heart I loved
　Our native trees the best.

And I have turnèd from orange trees
　In straightest orchard lines,
To lay my face in musky sprays
　Plucked from the wild grape vines.

The very earliest in spring
　Were golden willow blooms,
And there hummed busy honey bees,
　Amid the sweet perfumes.

There is a tree that groweth wild
   In many a lonely spot;
By purling stream, or in the sands,
   It seems to matter not.

And one of these grew on a knoll,
   'Twas branching, gnarled and low,
Hidden by poplars pointing high;
   And there I loved to go.

For, all around, a screen of vines
   Shut in and made it still;
And songsters in the reeds below,
   Fluttered and bathed at will.

'Twas only in the sweet springtime,
   A stranger's eyes might see
The secret of my preference
   For this strange little tree.

The trunk and branches, knotted, rough,
   Like withered twigs alway;
The foliage scant, devoid of grace,
   Less green than ashen gray.

But, in the springtime, if forgot,
   The early morning air,
The coming of the lilac blooms,
   The tidings sweet would bear.

So dainty sweet, yet soft warm winds
   Conveyed it far and wide;
And poplars tall, nor desert shrub,
   The lilacs now could hide.

So purely, rarely delicate,
  These lovely sprays appear,
As though soft clouds, wrought into lace,
  Had caught entangled here.

And so the while my lilac tree
  Its bride-like veiling wore,
I used to go, and each day deemed
  It fairer than before.

Yet, like so many other joys
  That to our lives are told,
I learned to love them where they were—
  To see and not to hold.

For so ethereal they seemed,
  That, with the tend'rest care,
They withered in the eager hands
  That won, but might not wear.

Yet resting on the turf beneath,
  Gazing up overhead,
I, through this heaven-broidered veil,
  Sweet intuitions read.

And though the few brief weeks of bloom
  For me too swiftly passed,
Their pure delight had wrought a charm
  Through time and change to last.

And so, for its sweet sake, oft times
  My visits still I made,
As faithful ones go from glad scenes
  To where the lost are laid.

*   *   *   *   *   *   *

I can but think that different kinds
   Bear spirits, each its own ;
Oft have I felt such influence
   In those that I have known.

The staunch old oak, the lonely pine
   In mountain solitudes,
The shrub that points the desert's dearth
   And nature's sullen moods.

The tree arrayed in mail of thorns
   Wards off all friendliness,
While these that blossom 'round our door
   Bring sense of happiness.

The vine climbs up as with caress,
   And wakes a fonder tone ;
These and all others speak to me
   In language each its own.

Shall I yet see that miracle—
   The word who can destroy?
That, when He comes, all flesh will speak
   And trees clap leaves for joy?

BETROTHED.

WHY is it, that through all the day
 And waking hours of night,
My thoughts run all the same sweet way,
 One path of calm delight?
A few short months ago, and we
 As strangers met and passed,
No thrill of joy awoke in me,
 No thought on me you cast.

But strangely, fate has caught and tied
 Together our life threads
In a sweet love knot, nor denied
 Friends' blessings on our heads.
Strangers a year ago, to-day
 I sit and slow recall
Our walk beneath the starry way
 And words your lips let fall.

Yet stay, my pencil! there may lean
 Some spirit reading this,
Whose envious power might intervene
 To part my life from his.
No further be the secret read,
 Until himself shall lay
His crown of love upon my head,
 To bless my life alway.

A WINTER EVENING.

CURTAIN out the stormy night,
Sit beside me while I read;
While before, the ruddy flames,
Leap and struggle as in pain;
Gloom and rain and wind without.
Warmth and light and love within,
Happy faces smiling 'round,
My heart like the ingle leaps and burns.
No happier hearth can there be found;
I bless God's love for this good home,
For shelter, happiness and friends.

THE ANSWER.

WHAT hast Thou given me, dear Lord?
    The words I did not speak,
But yet they entered in my heart
    By trial weary grown and weak.

Have I not given thee thyself,
    Thy life a broad new field,
Wherein, by earnest, watchful toil,
    Some wondrous work might be revealed?

Have I not given to thee sight?
  Before thine eyes unfold
Life's living lessons, leading on
  Thy steps to wonders yet untold.

Have I not given thee the right
  All good to emulate?
Naught shall withhold from thee the prize
  Thy soul may seek, though high and great.

Have I not given thee the right
  All living kind to bless,
And do my work, where want and woe
  Have wrought their deep distress?

Have I not given unto thee
  Some joy for every day?
Hast thou not had some loving one
  To walk with thee, whate'er the way?

Have I not given unto thee
  My promise true and sure,
To hear thy prayer, and be thy friend,
  Through all that thou may'st e'er endure?

Have I not given thee my word:
  When life and death are o'er,
To bring the faithful home again
  And send them from my side no more?

What other gift shall I bestow?
  Wouldst thou come home to me?
Has earth no bond to claim thy love?
  Would none be lonely missing thee?

Yes, and if I have weary grown,
    How could they keep the way?
To guide, or bear them in my arms,
    This heart, though faint, would turn and stay.

Dear Lord, grant for their sakes this boon,
    As on with them I go:
Look Thou upon Thy tender lambs
    And bid Thy winds less rudely blow.

THE ABODE OF THE MUSE.

My muse, may I entreat your ear?
    And would you deign to tell
Your most respectful worshiper,
    Where muses really dwell?

Always have I been grateful for
    Your visits, satisfied
With whatsoe'er your gracious mood
    My list'ning ear supplied.

And 'till to-day, I ne'er had thought
    Of asking anything,
Beyond whate'er it pleased yourself
    From fancy's realms to bring.

But curiosity, they say,
    Is part of woman's mind;
That there's a trace, whether she be
    Uncultured or refined.

And if its true it can't be helped,
　And if it shouldn't be,
I'm sure, my muse, you'll not think it
　Inquisitive of me.

For things I never thought about,
　Of course I do not care ;
But something that I want to know,
　Becomes a grave affair.

And, after thinking long of it,
　I said next time you came,
I'd nerve myself sufficiently
　The new idea to name.

So if it's fair to ask it, and
　You don't mind telling me,
I'll be the first to know, and all
　The rest will envious be.

If it's a secret, how can one
　Accustomed long to share
Her inmost thoughts with all the world,
　The wond'rous news forbear?

But if it is, rather than lose
　The answer, of course, I
Will, with the stern condition charged,
　Endeavor to comply.

And do they dwell in castles fair,
　In azure cloud-walled heights,
And have they always summer clime,
　And glowing moonlit nights?

And have they castes of rich and poor?
  I pray you, let me know;
And do they ride on winged steeds,
  As some declare is so?

And oh! I'd really like to ask
  One thing above the rest:
If whether man or womankind,
  They love to favor best?

Is there some secret order, which
  Has signs, by which you know
These poet-souls, although disguised
  And scattered here below?

And though I'm almost out of breath,
  And really very tired,
I'm wide awake to listen to
  The truth so long desired.

*   *   *   *   *   *   *

Thou child of earth, we come to thee
  From wond'rous realms afar,
Past azure fields and cloud-walled heights,
  And many a glowing star.

Our home is in that source of light
  From whence all good hath birth;
We bring to thee this precious gift
  To bless and gladden earth.

Around its charm, if sacred kept,
  The good and great will throng;
And raptured lips learn and repeat
  The beauty of the song.

Though thou hast sown thy gift with joy,
    Greater reward will come,
If lips shall yield their Maker praise,
    That, ere thy song, were dumb.

The rank we hold in that high court,
    Nor birth nor wealth ensures;
The soul's pure use of every good,
    It name and place secures.

Alike in ages of the past,
    Poetic flame has fired
The lips of prophets and of kings,
    And woman's heart inspired.

And when we come, where'er we chance
    To find a votary,
Though proud or humble be the home,
    There our abode will be.

Not oft in palace walls do we
    The poet-toiler find,
Vain pageantries leave season brief
    To search the inner mind.

Rather where busy industry,
    And earnest lives abound,
Where people live for truth and right,
    The muses' home is found.

E'en as the captive bird sometimes
    Forgets its cage and sings;
Also o'er all restraints and wrongs
    The poet's soul upsprings.

Nor dungeon's depth, and chilling gloom,
   Have quenched the glowing spark ;
And truth and beauty both have shone
   The brighter through the dark.

But dearest to the muse of all,
   Some sheltered, peaceful spot,
Where Nature's calm recalls the spell
   'Mid jarring scenes forgot.

And I have known the muse to walk
   The farmer's plow beside,
And whisper where, by vine-wreathed door,
   A maid her needle plied.

And I have known the muse to come
   To one who loneliest roamed,
Yet taught the lips of all the world,
   To sing of "Home, Sweet Home."

And once I knew of ruined walls
   Where rain and sleet crept in,
And winter winds wailed discord to
   The poet's heart within.

Nor mandate stern, nor misery,
   Can muse and minstrel part ;
The muses' kingdom 's all the world,
   Their home, the poet's heart !

HENRY W. LONGFELLOW.

In one room of the dear old home,
    Each side the fireplace,
Broad bookshelves, from the ceiling down,
    Filled and adorned the space.

On the left side a table stood,
    With father's desk and chair,
And on the right a quaint old chest
    Of magazines most rare.

Eclectics, Sartain's, Lady's Books,
    And others I searched through
For pictures ; skipping o'er Blackwood's,
    Reviews and Journals too.

On stormy days I loved to sit
    Within it at one end,
Contented, in this treasury,
    The afternoon to spend.

Above my head, on topmost shelf,
    I found a volume old,
Well read and very worn within,
    Bound all in red and gold.

The name—ah ! yes, a larger book
    Was farther down below ;
This was, perhaps, the poet's first,
    Published long years ago.

And so I said, this shall be mine,
    And when I've read it through,
The newer and the larger one,
    Perhaps, I shall read too.

I read it all, and then again,
    And when I read still more,
Each line to my unfolding mind
    A deeper meaning bore.

Through twenty years this volume small
    My heart's best choice remained;
Nor other poet e'er could win
    The height he had attained.

And pure as great his triumphs are,
    When even children bring
Their homage to his life's high work,
    As their best offering.

Children of Cambridge, ye will live
    Linked with his deathless fame;
Ye have immortalized your own,
    Wreathing with love his name.

O, true the spirit's whisperings,
    When years returning prove
A wider fame, a deeper love,
    In the world's heart unmoved.

O, rare that wreath of fame, wherein
    The nations each have brought
A laurel leaf, as for its own,
    To speak its tend'rest thought.

The Album.

❖ ─◆─ ❖

TO THE PORTRAIT OF E. R. S. S.

THOSE eyes are eyes of truth.
More beautiful than eyes of youth,
   Are these that softly shine;
That seem to turn from dreams
Of high and sacred themes,
   To answ'ring look in mine.

Royal thy spirit's grace,
And calm thy gentle face,
   Though restless all beside;
Thy soul in peace doth rest
Upon the surging breast
   Of life's tumultuous tide.

When storms around thee break,
Thy trusting hand doth take,
   Still closer, faith's white hand;
Nor clouds that hide the shore,
Nor waves that round thee roar,
   Can thy firm heart command.

The beauty of thy life,
Nor luxury, nor strife,
　　Could blemish, or destroy;
Through all, thy sacred aim
Has been, and is, the same—
　　Its labors all thy joy.

Earth's lowly homes to choose,
To gather and diffuse
　　Wisdom and love therein;
Virtue and law to teach,
And bounteous aid to each,
　　Thy chosen work has been.

Thy faithful steps have sought
The scattered, to them brought,
　　From thy soul's treasury,
Of good and joy such store;
They who loved thee before,
　　Regard thee reverently.

And love halos thy name,
A queen might stoop to claim,
　　So pure and true its worth;
No name that poet's sing
A warmer thought can bring—
　　Our first of all the earth.

TO Z. D. Y.

" There is none like unto thee."

———

WHENE'ER the record of my years,
   In solitude I slow recall,
Thy name in changeless light appears,
   Shedding its brightness over all.

Remembrance of thy love has been,
   In trial-hour, a strength to me;
Though blest the hour, or bright the scene,
   No other friend more dear could be.

If, when the higher life we gain,
   Thy friendship pure I still may hold;
How blest to speak, in language plain,
   The love, in this, can ne'er be told.

———◆▷▶◀◀◆———

TO M. I. H.

———

IN retrospection I review
   Thy life and labors, honored friend,
And from a heart sincere, would fain
   This humble tribute to thee send.

The kindly words thou gavest me,
   Like precious gems worthily set,
I wear within my heart alway,
   And never may their charm forget.

Thy words of wisdom, deeds of love,
   Have strengthened and inspired those
Bowed down in grief beneath the weight
   Of earnest need, and spirit woes.

How blest the power thou dost hold,
   God's truths to teach, and joy to give
To thine own race; making their lives
   The happier that thou dost live.

TO E. B. W.

ACCOMPANYING A WATCH PRESENTED BY HER FRIENDS.

Around thy name, where'er 'tis heard,
   What pleasant thoughts responsive rise!
They who have known thee longest, best,
   Thy worth and friendship dearest prize.
Thy soul unfolding like a flower,
   Sheltered from rude winds all its youth,
Grew strong and fearless, and took on
   Faith's armor in the cause of truth.

Through persecution, want and death,
   Thy spirit's strength has never quailed,
Nor worldly homage thee beguiled;
   Thy loyal faith has never failed.
Into how many hearts and homes
   The *Exponent* goes, a welcome guest!
It has wrought good in city homes
   And the far settler's cabin blest.

And missionaries far away,
　Have turned with smiling eyes to greet
The little messenger that came
　With precious news from home replete.
If all the hearts that turn to you
　In kindly thought, to-night could come,
How many strangers we should greet!
　'Twould need a hall, to find them room.

And so a few of us have sought
　To demonstrate, dear friend, to you
The high regard and love of all
　Who know your life and service true.
And as time softly ticks along,
　May he sometimes within your ear
Whisper a word in memory
　Of these to-night assembled here.

E. B. F.

A ROYAL ancestry was there,
Her home was noble, broad and fair;
And she, in youth's sweet holiday,
Wore not a care to wish away.

They looked upon her as she dreamed,
Her life a favored daughter's seemed;
Yet lingered, as they turned to go,
Some newer favor to bestow.

Then one sang softly as she slept,
And in her dreams she caught and kept
The soul of music in her heart,
No more through life with it to part.

Another sat beside, and traced
In lines of beauty, scene and face,
Till (was she sleeping?) she had won
The angel's pencil for her own.

Still others to her dreaming ear,
Brought legends rare for her to hear;
And each one, as she read or sung,
Spoke in her own sweet mother tongue;

And lent her, ne'er on earth to lose,
Their native languages to use.
One touched her hand, and from that hour
Pain yielded unto her its power.

They draped her with a gentle grace
That time might never more efface;
She wore it with unconscious smile,
Yet quiet dignity, the while.

They kissed and left her, still to keep
The gifts they gave her in her sleep.
O, blest the treasures angels bring!
The riches that ne'er take to wing.

Jewels that in the spirit worn,
The outward woman may adorn;
That freely given, grow no less,
And by their usage charm and bless.

TO S. M. K.

WHERE Zion's daughters true are found,
  The elect bearers of His word,
And holy joy and peace surround,
  Thy face is seen, thy voice is heard.

Where'er our people's lives are known,
  Thine honored name hath reached the heart;
Thy history twining with their own,
  Ne'er wavering from theirs apart.

Within the record of thy days,
  A kingdom's founding thou hast known;
And temples builded to God's praise,
  Have shown the pathway to His throne.

How well to worthy ones endeared,
  Thine album's pages, witness bear;
And grateful, I, 'mid these revered
  And noble names, a place to share.

May all thy years to come know peace,
  Angels illume and guard thy way,
And added triumphs still increase
  Thy praise, till resurrection day.

TO H. T. K.

A NOBLE lady claims of me
A task, whereto I smiling turn,
A task of honor, opening
Her album's pages for my pen.

Of noble spirit, culture rare,
. Of earnest purpose and pure life ;
A mind whose tablets might reveal
The sage's thought, the poet's sigh,
With here and there a vision fair
Of that unseen blest home beyond ;
Of truths by angel influence taught.
And o'er her titles, too, the names
Of wife and mother sweetly shine.

Worthy 'mong names revered to write,
Among names sacred Scriptures bear,
Women forever reverenced !
Hereafter, history's page will bear
Her name among its shining ones ;

It will be said of her: She lived
Far back in those dark stormy days
When God's true kingdom, new restored,
Was weak, and jealous evil strong.
When prophets bled ; and men of state—
In ignorance, as dark as when
Grey-haired Galileo suffered for
His truths ; or cruel priests held rule—
Made laws to make a people's free,
Great men, of holy lives and aims,

Serfs to their equals in the land,
And false to Him who, leading them,
Made them a kingdom and a light
Of peace, above a jealous world.

She was among that band who rose
When "Cullom's Bill" woke into life
A kingdom's women to a deed—
Search history's record vainly o'er
For one will match—as grand, as pure!
An equal harmony of thought,
An equal charity of heart,
Whence selfishness was all erased;
Hearts that for love of womankind,
Hearts that for love of chastity,
Reached out the hand to women true,
Help unto love and honor both.
Dividing home, love, comfort, all!
An impulse that thrilled through the land,
Echoing back from north and south,
Where'er the hateful tidings sped;
Scorning the blackened hand that reached
Its broken reed, its promise false;
And hurled back, in the giver's face,
With scorn and pity for the mind
That bred such offspring to the light.
A race of women who could choose
'Twixt God's commands and man's, and say,
"Thy God, thy home, thy grave be mine."

With depth of mind for earnest truths,
Yet charity for rhyme or tale,
How blest for me such friend to find!
And I so hidden, so afraid

Of venture, e'en by tongue or pen!
How did you find my soul within,
That sat so long behind the veil
Where many passed and nothing saw?
And took me kindly by the hand,
And walked beside me in the ways
My spirit trod so long alone.

And honored, I, that in that shrine
So near the heart, the album's page,
You give me place beside your friends.
There shall I sit while years go on,
Working their change for good or ill,
While life unfolds, or death enfolds,
Shall still be near you, nor grow changed.

TO A BEAUTIFUL DOCTOR, (E. R. S.)

Accompanying a ring, presented by the Y. L. M. I. A.

THE Father sitting on His throne,
    Searching the hearts of all,
Whose prayers, before the golden steps,
    Like precious perfumes fall,

From out His boundless treasuries
    Some fitting blessing sought,
Answering those who, trusting Him,
    Their heart's petitions brought.

So many and so wonderful,
  They could not all be told ;
Yet in the hands He gives them, may
  Increase an hundredfold.

And unto one of lovely face
  And pure and gentle soul,
He gave a wand of wondrous power
  In her fair hand to hold.

Where helpless lie, in darkened rooms,
  The sick and suffering,
·This blessed gift floods all with light,
  And pain and grief take wing.

Within this golden circle small,
  An emblem fit is found
Of thy worth and thy purity,
  And friendship's endless round.

And while you wear it, may it bring
  Before your thought, dear friend,
The circle of true hearts, whose love
  For you will know no end.

ADDRESSED TO G. R.

Out of the darkness cometh light,
  And out of trial, strength,
Though the season of God's purposes
  Drags wearily its length.

Since first the gift, eternal truth,
  From heaven to earth was brought,
At the blessed sound, opposing hosts
  Have ceasless warfare wrought.

And they who seek to win the crown,
  Erewhile the cross must bear;
But though in the gloom of prison cell
  God sends His angels there.

And all the efforts of His foes
  Rebound but to their shame;
But trials borne by the Saint proved true
  Add honors to His name.

Receive in thine own heart to-night,
  The joy that each extends,
Wishing thee long years of life and peace
  'Mid children, wives and friends.

THE WEIGHT OF A WORD.

WAIT, O love!
Awhile no answer speak,
Until the flame has died away
Upon thy tender cheek.
No pride that ever burned,
But from its ashes yet
Will rise the haunting phantoms
Of love, and love's regret.

Wait, O friend!
And wouldst thou cast aside
By just a breath, the happy past,
And one so true and tried?
Canst thou another find
To fill the vacant place?
And canst thou shut out from thy heart
The old familiar face?

Mother, wait!
Shalt thou, who knowest best
The inmost depths of that young heart,
Its frail endurance test?
If thou, the mother, prove
In judgment swift and stern,
To whom shall he, in coming years,
For tender mercy turn?

Wait, O child!
Thou dost not know how deep,
Unloving words sink in the heart
And haunt the dreamer's sleep.

Thy parent's love for thee
　Notes every look and tone,
And age will turn to early years
　When other scenes have flown.

　　Man of wealth!
Thy word a moment weigh;
Perchance thine aid, a fellow man
　From dark despair may stay.
Hast thou denied him work?
　Thou hast denied him bread;
And He who weighs the desp'rate act,
　Weighs too the prayer he plead.

　　Just one word!
The scale may bear and turn.
O ye that speak it, think of those
　Who lean that word to learn.
O joy! if, in response,
　The heart may upward rise;
O sorrow! if, beneath its weight,
　A life's sweet gladness dies.

AFTER TRIAL.

COME, O griefs, that plough the mind,
　Tearing heart through root and vein;
I can smile if I but find
　Some new strength through pain.

But, O heart, I must bestow
  One stern charge e'en now on thee,
Though soft rays beam through thy woe:
  As when scathed tree—

Quiv'ring yet with lightning's stroke,
  Glittering in its veil of tears,
Bright, although its form be broke,
  Living yet appears—

Friends may raise and bind anew
  Riven, helpless, dying form ;
Take not such a hope to you
  In this hush of storm.

Retrospection of dead joys,
  Hopes deferred, may wear away.
Courage! faith in human voice,
  Faith for better day !

But the heart, aye, upward springs
  From the step that bent it low ;
And e'en wrung by nature, clings
  To hope's promise bow.

And philosophy will creep
  In through crevices, unseen,
And beam, sun-like, while we weep,
  Calming all the scene.

Do the maple leaves make 'plaint
  While, beneath the woodman's wound,
All her sweetness yields? 'till faint,
  Droop her branches down?

Does the earth at heart grow cold
　'Neath the miner's blow that thrills,
Wresting forth her gems and gold,
　Scarring all her hills?

Were the vintage never crushed,
　We should never taste the wine ;
Were the 'plaints of trial hushed,
　Tangled still would intertwine,

'Round the spirit pure, the roots
　Of the evil inly born ;
While life's habit, like a mask,
　O'er its truth is worn.

Oh, my angel! lead me so,
　Through this world so strange and wide,
Though through trials deep I go,
　I may reach thy side.

THE VICTORY.

WAIT thou awhile, dear friend, and they
　Who have misjudged thee so
Will learn the wrong thou hast endured,
　And their own error know.

Lips that repeat thy blame at first
　Will their confusion see,
The true in heart amend their deed
　And love and honor thee.

Secure and lasting is the faith
  That right and patience win,
And joyful is the victory
  If thou canst say within:

I have o'ercome mine enemy,
  Henceforth, unto the end,
His arm, his tongue, no more I fear;
  I have made him my friend.

ENVY.

NAY, thou dark shade, there ne'er should be
A place within my breast for thee.
Gainst thine inferiors, 'twere shame
For thee to cherish envious blame.
Let those above thee, stimulate
Thy mind their worth to emulate.

THE STRANGER IN OUR HOME.*

THERE'S a stranger in the house;
  With an anxious heart she came.
Let her lot, O, gentle lady,
  Thy deep thought a moment claim.

*—Suggested by remarks of Pres. Jos. E. Taylor, at a ladies' meeting.

In thy words let kindly feeling
    Be revealed in every tone;
Bear in mind while friends surround thee,
    She is here apart, and lone.

Let her feel thou hast for her
    Worthy, womanly regard,
And the toiler, in her gladness
    Will not find her lot so hard.
Hast thou sought what motive sent
    This young stranger to thy door?
Has she left a dear home's threshold
    For a life ne'er braved before?

Then, when busy day is done,
    Her young lonely heart will miss
The sweet gladness of those evenings,
    And the loving good night kiss.
Dost thou know, when the long night
    Brings sweet sleep to thine so dear,
If she, restless, on her pillow,
    Homesick, sheds the silent tear?

Is she toiling in our midst
    To relieve a parent's care?
Is't that little brothers, sisters,
    Added gifts and joys may share?
Shall we count her station low,
    Or her spirit's work as less
Than our own, if she has power
    Weaker ones to aid and bless?

Or without these, shall we then
    Her life's loneliness ignore?
I'st the same, with or without her—
    Just a tool, and nothing more?
Shall we be too proud to seek
    For what homely garb may hide:
For the soul, that through this wide world
    Is the lone life's faithful guide?

Did she come across the sea,
    Leaving all she loved behind?
Was it told her that among us
    She a welcoming would find?
Have we chilled a young heart's faith
    'Till our sister turned away,
To the kinder voice of strangers
    Who have led her steps astray?

O, the stranger in our homes!
    Every one of these has had
Just such mother-love's caressing
    As has made our own babes glad.
From love learned in mother-arms,
    Ne'er can cease the heart to crave
Kindliness from fellow creatures
    All life's pathway to the grave.

Shall we call her sister, then,
    Where we meet to praise and pray,
Yet assume a diff'rent bearing
    In our home lives day by day?
And perchance the stranger yet
    Through the favor of God's will,
May be chosen from our household,
    Honored place in life to fill.

Give the words of kindness, then,
　To the stranger while we may;
And, like "bread cast on the waters,"
　When has passed by many a day,
Waves of time from farther shores
　Will, returning, bear to thee
Fruit from seed thou hadst forgotten,
　Nurtured in her memory.

THE BETRAYED.

THAT I had forgotten thee,
　When thou dost need me more,
Now in thine hour of loneliness,
　Than ever thou didst before?

That I who had love for thee
　When friends around thee smiled,
Could from my heart erase all thought
　Of thee and thy hapless child?

Too often in our own race,
　Do we resemblance find,
To those who rend and hunt to death
　The wounded of their own kind.

But lift thy head and smile ;
　For grief doth but endear
The lone one to those faithful friends,
　That trial has proved sincere.

And when thou wouldst look around,
　For one of these to see;
When thou wouldst speak thy grief, or weep,
　Then come, dear friend, to me.

THE SONGS OF HOME.

Across the garden carelessly
　The zephyr soft doth bring,
In broken snatches, a sweet lay
　My mother used to sing.

And from her lips, like sacred joy,
　Each charmed cadence fell;
And one sang with her, deepening
　The words' and music's spell.

O, idle singer, sing no more
　That dear old song to-day;
O, thoughtless lips, I pray you wait
　'Till I am far away.

Whate'er they sang, it was enough
　For me, enrapt to hear;
Its burden, to my inmost soul,
　Seemed real, and close anear.

I saw the skies of Italy,
　And nightingales sang sweet;
Gondolas passed 'neath moonlight clear,
　And waves washed at my feet.

I heard the anthem of the sea
  Echo along the shore,
I saw its billows white with wrath
  And heard its thund'rous roar.

Songs of the forest!   I could feel
  The breeze across my face,
And heard the whirr of wings, as rode
  The hunters of the chase.

I trembled 'neath the gloomy pines,
  And heard the torrent's fall,
And echoing from peak to peak,
  The fearless Switzer's call.

I heard them sing of lofty deeds
  By noble ones, and pure;
And I felt strong in heart and soul
  All trial to endure.

They sang of love, and, by the charm,
  The light of love became
No passing dream by fancy wrought!
  But sacred, deathless flame.

Yet could I, from the past, to-day,
  Evoke but one of all,
I'd hear again one sacred hymn,
  And that dear group recall.

O, lips that gave it beauty, life,
  Do ye up there forget
The rapture of those sacred strains,
  Or do ye sing them yet?

As sometimes stars, unlooked for, fall,
　　Across the heavens clear,
So through commingled daily sounds
　　That hymn sometimes I hear.

O, dear ones! when ye sing in joy,
　　Do ye remembrance bear
Of earthly harmonies, and these
　　Who in thy love had share?

O, idle singer, sing no more
　　That dear old song to-day!
O, careless lips, I pray you wait
　　'Till I am far away!

JUST TO KISS HIM.

SUMMONED beside her dying bed,
　　In silence stern he came,
As though too proud e'en yet to speak
　　In loving tone, her name.

Before her eyes the filmy veil,
　　That shuts earth's sights away,
Was falling softly; little time
　　Was left sweet words to say.

The eager eyes looked all in vain
　　Responsive love to meet;
Yet, o'er the pang, with strength sublime,
　　Her soul rose pure and sweet.

She raised her arms and clasped his neck,
  The old love to recall ;
And whispered, with the failing breath :
  "To kiss him"—that was all.

Vain were the barriers of pride
  Against that parting breath ;
And vain the prayer that thrilled his heart,
  Upon the ear of death.

AN INCIDENT IN WALES, 1880.

SLOW and weary, through the dusk,
  Ere the morning light broke through,
Bearing each a feeble light,
  Came the colliers, two by two.

Night, with steps soft as the dew,
  Brought to these no blessed sleep ;
Toilers for their fellow-men,
  In the black pits, damp and deep.

Could one, looking on them, dream
  They were babes once, sweet and fair—
These with faces sullen, rough,
  From the life-lot that they bear?

Like some troops of spirits dark,
  Through the chilling morn they came,
Gloomy, silent, in the bonds
  Of a life through years the same.

Then, before their path, uprose
  Through the thick veil of the gloom,
Like a vision, figures strange,
  As though risen from the tomb.

Yet no fear thrilled through the hearts
  Of these blackened, hopeless men,
As they paused a moment only,
  And moved slowly on again.

'Twas the famished! young and aged,
  Who from sleepless beds had come
To await, from these poor miners,
  The night luncheon's crust and crumb.

Worse, by far, than phantom steps,
  That through ruined halls may glide,
These despairing, living creatures
  That stood by the highway side!

Angels, that in witness stand,
  How can ye your silence keep,
Over selfish pride and splendor,
  While the helpless, suffering, weep?

Angels, do ye record bear
  Of these wrongs which men have wrought?
How for gold and station striving
  These poor lives are counted naught?

O, ye mighty ones! whose hands
  The great Master's riches hold,
How shall ye make answer to Him
  When your lives and deeds are told?

If ye have not ministered
  Unto these He sent to thee,
When He comes to judge His servants
  What will the dread sentence be?

Blessed, ye, to hold in keeping,
  Power, life's evils to remove,
And while blessing fellow-creatures,
  Thy soul's love for Him to prove.

Dim the splendor, false the glory,
  Of these paltry courts of earth,
If held in selfish existence,
  Lacking deeds of noble worth.

BABY'S TIRED.

HERE comes baby, wearily,
  Drooping head and footsteps slow,
All the little chatter hushed;
  What has tired the baby so?

I had said, only last night,
  That his life knew not a shade;
Loving ones for him, each day,
  A fair holiday had made.

Straightway to my chair he comes—
  "Baby's tired," and he lays
On my knee his curly head,
  Looking out with dreamy gaze

On the group beneath the tree,
  Stream and sward, and scattered toy;
Where's the charm gone? Not a thing
  Tempts the eye of my sweet boy.

Has it come to this so soon?
  Could not care delay awhile?
Why! these little rosy feet
  Could not travel half a mile.

Nay, I think it most unjust,
  Time should hasten on like this!
What a miser! you might think
  Little heads he'd sometimes miss.

Ah, but no! he counts these too,
  Taxes each one with a care;
He'll bring burdens for these shoulders,
  Just as fast as they can bear.

No! I cannot help resent;
  Tell me, what has baby done, .
Even joys should weigh so heavy
  Ere his life has scarce begun?

"Take him?" Tell me, where's the tyrant
  I'd obey as quick as this?
And his head's so heavy that he
  Lifts his hand up to be kissed.

Just an hour ago these fingers
  Reached for everything in sight,
Nay, 'tis treason e'en to name it
  Of this hand so still and white;

For the last faint thought expressed
  By these precious finger tips,
Was a plea for love—love only,
  From these same half blaming lips.

Weariness and joys together,
  Baby has forgotten quite;
Yet down in his deep sweet slumbers,
  See, he holds my finger tight.

This, the time when we two only
  Comprehend a secret spell,
Gentler far than look or whisper,
  Peace and love no speech could tell.

Thou, the link 'twixt me and heaven!
  Dost thou still remembrance keep
Of its glory? yet thou turnest
  To thy mother's arms to sleep.

Thou and I and angels, darling,
  Meet together in this hour
Where all creatures bow in wonder,
  Hushed before their Maker's power.

FOUR MEN.

GAZING so long, never winking,
  I thought I would like to know
Of what grave thing she was thinking
  That seemed to puzzle her so.

And demurely made answer then,
  To me, the little maiden:
"I was thinking, there are two men—
  Bad ones, Jack Frost and Satan.

"But I don't much mind these bad ones,"
  She added after a pause;
"For there are two very good ones:
  Heavenly Father and Santa Claus."

POLITE SLANG.

I KNEW an honored lady friend,
  Who had an extreme, earnest dread
Of careless words, as though their use
  To downward paths most surely led.
And so fastidious was her taste,
  Young ladies had to guarded be,
Lest they, forgetful, used such words.
  As met with her antipathy.

And once it chanced that she rehearsed
  Some deed our honest scorn might claim;
And I in sympathy replied,
  "It truly was an awful shame."
What had I done? Her very soul
  To its remotest depth was stirred!
"O, don't say awful, my dear girl—
  Indeed, it is an AWFUL word!"

Her good advice I ne'er forgot,
  Yet often hear, day after day,
Phrases by custom sanctioned, that
  Might almost take her breath away.
I often wonder if she has
  Grown used to slang, or whether yet
Her face wears that astonished look
  That mine on that occasion met.

What would she think to hear Miss Brown,
  As soon as plaudits cease to ring,
Pronounce *Basso Profundo*, as
  "Too awful sweet for anything."
And when to her admiring friends,
  Miss Brown with raptured air exclaims,
She "never, never heard before,
  Such awfully ecstatic strains."

And then Miss Brown goes on to say,
  In language this time scarce so rash:
"He had the awfullest black eyes,"
  And such an "awful cute moustache."
He wore an "awful splendid" ring,
  Also an "awful lovely" suit;
And (this time I believe 'twas true)
  He wore an "awful little boot."

And anxious to outdo herself,
  Brings out this hapless, same adverb,
To make you comprehend 'twas all
  "Perfectly, awfully superb."
Could but *Basso Profundo* hear
  These criticisms to his face,
Would he still with expression sing,
  Or let some other fill his place?

I heard Fernando one day read,
  To Dollie, some poetic line :
She scanned her rings and said it was
  "Just quite too awfully sublime."
A lady called upon a friend
  And chanced the little one to see ;
"Why, isn't baby growing fast?"
  "Yes, he is growing 'fearfully.'"

If some wise one should e'er compile
  The vagrant phrases now in use,
What lesson would the showing teach,
  Of fallen taste and word-abuse.
E'en in the *boudoir* of the fair,
  Appears the evil spirit slang :
The tress that waves on beauty's brow,
  By dainty lips is termed a "bang."

If these lips yet must give account
  For ev'ry idle word let fall,
For hasty words we may atone,
  But slang will shame us most of all.
Then gather words as thou wouldst flowers,
  Nor let these weeds thy spirit stain ;
The first will deck thee fair and sweet,
  The last makes beauty all in vain.

THE POET'S VISION.

THE poet stood alone in thought,
　　All life seemed dull and slow,
And duty's steps at every turn
　　To meet a sullen foe.

The sounds of earth broke on his ear
　　In harsh discordant tones,
He turned from folly's revelry
　　And met misfortune's moans.

He missed the faces of his friends,
　　And, 'round his soul, a spell
Of loneliness, doubt and despair,
　　Like gloomy shadows fell.
He looked abroad—earth's creatures all
　　Walked 'neath the evil shade
Where might and wrong, 'gainst truth and right,
　　Their larger hosts arrayed.

Nor innocence, nor purity,
　　Nor noble natures, won
Defense or mercy from their hate,
　　That left no wrongs undone.
"O, earth!" he cried, "thy fairest scenes
　　May not the vision hide
Of human wrongs that, shaming man,
　　His boasted power deride.

"Upon thy bosom leaves unfold,
　　Uplifting to the sun
The growth and service God ordained,
　　Until their lives are done.

But man, the highest of His works,
   Spends, in indifferent days,
The seasons and earth's treasuries,
   Scarce yielding Him his praise.

"In towering strength, from year to year,
   The Upas flaunts o'erhead,
And 'round our feet, in ranker growth,
   Ensnaring evils spread.
Indifferent, in selfish ease,
   His favored sons deride
The cry that swells from wretched haunts,
   Where want and woe abide.

"Before the overwhelming force
   Of evils that appall,
From earnest hands that strive in vain,
   The feeble weapons fall.
And must e'en these, in dumb despair,
   Yield to the threatening foe,
And swell the ranks of that dread power,
   Through deeper crimes to go?"

He looked, and, scattered far and wide,
   Saw spirits fair and good,
That with unshaken faith and will
   All power of sin withstood.
"O, would my soul might reach to these,
   And unto each one bear
A sign of hope, a staff of strength,
   To lead them from despair!"

Then in each gentle face he saw
  A soul-light, pure and clear,
That brought sweet peace to all who came
  Within its sacred sphere.
Lives that, in patience suffering,
  Had not their help denied
To fellow-creatures that, oppressed,
  Sank by the highway side.

"Have I in weak despondence strayed
  Aside, with ling'ring feet,
While these, distressed on every hand,
  No duty failed to meet?
Weaker the dark and restless hosts
  Of might and error grow,
When such as these, with tireless faith,
  Their sacred purpose show.

"The soul's work, wrought in purity,
  Becomes a tower high,
That, planted on foundations firm,
  May storms and time defy.
O, souls, through trials purified,
  Count not your suffering loss,
Ye have become the gold refined,
  Untarnished by the dross."

He caught the spirit of their lives,
  And saw, with raptured eyes,
The wondrous triumphs that they won
  Like holy visions rise;
The cries of martyrs changed to psalms,
  The foeman's cries to pain;
The sullen clouds, 'gainst radiant skies,
  Their shadows massed in vain.

All life a sacred drama seemed,
    Where, passing in review,
All creatures filled appointed place,
    For purpose grand and true.
Then, from his lips the sacred joy
    Broke forth in wondrous song;
And falling winds, the grand refrain
    Repeated far and long.

The poet woke—the dream had passed,
    But in his spirit, still,
He kept its lesson—sacredly,
    His mission to fulfill.

A LOST THOUGHT.

O, WHAT was that lost thought?
    And where can it have flown?
The veriest will-o'-the-wisp,
    I've e'er heard of, or known.
While bending o'er my task,
    This thought came to my mind,
And, pleased that it had come to me
    A guardian to find,

I said, "Now, very soon
    I'll stop and take the time
To frame the beauty of this theme
    Well as I may, in rhyme.

For duties have first claim,
    Or everything goes wrong;
And a good dinner's prized above
    The rhymer's sweetest song."

And so when all was done,
    And I sat down at last,
This guest of mine was far away,
    A phantom of the past!
In vain I conjured back
    The morning's dull routine,
Of anxious plans and homely tasks,
    With fancies slipped between;

'Twas gone—nought could recall
    A clue by which to trace
The form, or name, or spirit of
    The lost thought's transient grace.
I know that it was bright:
    It won an answ'ring smile;
Was't earnest haste, or light caprice,
    Forbade it wait awhile?

You say, "it's not worth while
    To care;" but then, you see,
What might console you very well,
    Wont do at all for me.
After I've had a hint
    Of some fine, new idea,
I don't feel quite resigned to let
    The secret disappear!

O, climbing swaying vines!
　　Say, did I drop a word?
I pray you, by your fragrant breath,
　　Remind me what you heard.
O, straying, idle wind!
　　If, in your sun-lit track
You find the mystic wanderer,
　　O, bring the truant back.

O, bird, and bee, and brook!
　　Can you not help to find
The trifler, that brought smiles, and left
　　A mystery behind?
But whisp'ring leaves, nor wind,
　　Nor bird, nor brook have met
In all their paths, the fickle guest
　　That haunts my spirit yet.

Of all the arrant wights,
　　Unpunished, and uncaught,
The most vexatious, fleetest winged,
　　I know—is a lost thought!

THEIR INFLUENCE.

DISPIRITED, I laid aside
　　My busy pen, and thought,
How feeble will these efforts seem
　　When critics' eyes have sought
The errors out from every page,
　　And through their columns show
The public all the weaknesses
　　At one grand pencil blow.

And yet, the work I had begun
　My hand could not resign,
I thought of those whose kindly words
　Prompted this task of mine ;
And, for their sakes, though longing so
　To turn from pen and book,
I opened one, on faces fair
　Of gifted ones to look.

Had these attained the envied heights
　Unwearied, and without
That grave unrest that stays the step,
　And shades the heart with doubt?
Had these e'er heard, in strange surprise
　(As idle winds will bring
Upon their pinions, soft and low,
　Notes one afar will sing),

Words that with heavy meaning fell
　Upon the shrinking soul,
'Till vain regrets and blinding tears,
　Rose spite of all control?
Had these, rememb'ring weaker ones,
　Turned to the toil again,
And, trembling, laid their work beside
　The grander works of men ?

Looking on them, an influence
　Reached like resistless flame,
As though from out their charmed sphere
　They called my place and name.
O, faces dear ! ye brought to me
　A strength, a joy untold !
The pilgrim took the staff once more,
　To reach that far off goal.

PROSPECT HILL,

SALT LAKE CITY.

BBHIND, the noble mountains rise,
  The valley spreads below,
And from the brow, far down, I see
  The foaming torrent's flow.
A footbridge spans it here and there,
  And, sheltered by the hill,
I see and hear the waterfall
  And the old rustic mill.

But from this point the eye commands
  The landscape, miles around;
The Lake to right, the Fort to left,
  And at your feet the town;
The garden homes, the fields and groves,
  The Jordan's silver tide;
And iron horse that, thund'ring, speeds
  Through meadows stretching wide.

'Tis here the stranger tourists come
  To view and ne'er forget,
The garden in the desert made,
  A joy and wonder yet!
Here oft, when winter scarce has gone,
  They bring the feeble too,
As though to gather hope and strength
  From this enchanting view.

And, soon as leaves and mosses green,
  And wild flowers, spring in sight,
The children throng to fill their arms
  With treasures sweet and bright.

And I have sometimes even seen
   A solitary pair
Stand silent here while moonlight made
   The landscape strangely fair.

How oft this heart, when sad and weak,
   Has wandered here to find,
From healthful breeze and lovely scene,
   A balm and peace of mind.
Thou point of beauty! there's a charm
   E'en in thy name for me;
Thou hast made part of one year's page
   Within my history.

Here have I come with heart oppressed
   By hopes so oft deferred;
And here in silence thrilled with joy
   With these at last conferred.
May grander bards hereafter bring
   Their tributes unto thee,
Nor find a height within this vale
   That shall thy rival be.

"A WHITE LIE."

"KITTIE, I must not be disturbed,
   No matter who comes to-day!
From callers and from vexing cares
   I'm going to slip away,
And, in the farthest attic room,
   Have a quiet holiday."

"And would you please to tell me, ma'am,
   Whatever I am to do,
When your friends come, as sure they will,
   Inquiring just for you?
For some might want to wait awhile,
   And I know who'd do it, too!"

" 'Engaged' wont do, I know it well;
   Now, between you and I,
I've a good mind (just for this once),
   A common plan to try;
Just tell them that I'm 'not at home,'
   'Twill be only a 'white lie!' "

The evening came ; refreshed and pleased,
   She sat by her bright fire-side,
And glanced around the cheerful room
   With worthy, wifely pride ;
And turned to hear a coming step,
   With joy she did not hide.

His step was hurried, face was pale,
   "Dear, where were you gone to-day?
A messenger came thrice for you,
   But all the girl could say
In answer to inquiry, was,
   That you had gone away.

"Your girlhood's friend, sweet Mary Lee,
   With piteous language plead
That they should find and bring you, love,
   Beside her dying bed.
They sought in vain, no—'tis too late,
   Sweet Mary Lee is dead!"

A white lie? No! her heart proclaimed
　　The words of darkest dye.
And that long day's sweet stolen joy
　　Died out with despairing cry,
In anguish o'er the plea denied
　　By a masked, and real lie.

——— ♦ ———

JACQUELINE.

The great trees spread their branches wide,
　　The sun scarce fell between,
And homeward, came adown the road,
　　Marie and Jacqueline.
Marie, rose-cheeked and beautiful,
　　A child but twelve years old;
Adown her shoulders fell her hair
　　Like silk, and fair as gold.

From Jacqueline's pure, earnest eyes,
　　The soul looked forth unmarred;
Her brow was white, but one fair cheek
　　Was strangely stained and scarred.
"Tell us, dear Jacqueline," said one
　　Who walked beside the two,
"The story of the wolf that came
　　To Marie and to you."

Then gentle Jacqueline looked down,
　　And Marie raised her head,
As looking in a saint's sweet face,
　　"Yes, tell her, dear," she said.

"'Twas years ago, and Marie, here,
  Was but an infant child;
Between us and the village rose
  A forest dark and wild.

"And in the winter, the farm folks,
  When they had need to go,
Would go together through the woods,
  Across the frozen snow.
And once, when mother had to go,
  Before she went away,
She brought our neighbor, Marguerite,
  To spend with me the day.

"The day passed merrily enough,
  But when the sun was down
We stiller grew, and often turned
  Toward the far-off town.
We talked in whispers, by the fire,
  And silence round us crept,
For Marie, here, just six months old,
  Within her cradle slept.

"Would mother not be coming soon?
  'Twas growing very dark;
We heard no sound of whip or wheels,
  But, far off, a wolf's bark.
Then Marguerite grew pale, and wept,
  But did not dare to go
Out through the dark, and rising wind,
  Across the frozen snow.

"Above the dismal wind we heard
  The wolf's bark nearer still,
And then his steps upon the snow
  Close to our own door sill,

Then Marguerite fell on her knees,
    And I grew sick and weak.
He pressed the latch from off the door
    Ere we could move or speak.

"The icy wind rushed in like death,
    And from the outside gloom,
With glaring eyes, a hungry wolf
    Stepped just within the room.
He snuffed, then trotted 'cross the floor
    To where she sleeping lay;
My friend fell shrieking, and I saw
    Him bear Marie away!

"I did not scream or cry for help,
    But reached and caught a knife
And followed him with but one thought—
    To save the baby's life!
I knew I clasped him 'round the neck,
    I knew we struggled long,
I heard his teeth gnash in my flesh,
    And Marie crying strong.

"And that was all I knew just then,
    But when I woke, 'twas light,
And mother's tears were falling on
    My face in wild delight.
They brought the baby to my side,
    That I her face might see;
I could not understand their joy,
    'Twas like a dream to me.

"Day after day passed on, for me
    I scarcely dared to speak;
Yet sometimes wondered why my arms
    Were sore, and I so weak.

And when at last, they told me how
   They found us in the snow,
The black wolf dying, I alive,
   And Marie crying so ;

"I did not care for pain or scars,
   But cried for joy, that she
Was spared to bless our humble home,
   Our treasure still to be."
Said Marie, (tears were in her eyes),
   "Sweeter to me by far,
Than face of saint or lady grand,
   This one that bears the scar."

THE HAUNTED ROOM.

" THIS is a pleasant room," you say;
   My friend, you do not know
'Tis haunted, though it looks so bright;
   And yet, in truth, 'tis so.
For, though I come from busy scenes,
   And think to rest me here,
I scarce compose myself before
   I feel them draw anear.
They crowd around my homely chair,
   Against my face they lean ;
Through broken dreams adown my sleep,
   These spirits flit between.

They come, though I, with broom in hand,
   Their influence defy ;
I lay it down and listen while
   The morning hour goes by.

Though I'm on some new dress intent
　(You'd think that would dispel
Their power), yet my needle falls
　The while they weave their spell.

You look on me with wond'ring eyes
　As though you almost thought
My reason doubtful, and that you
　On dang'rous ground were caught.
Dismiss that look, my friend, I'll prove
　To you that every guest
Is harmless, and is welcome too;
　Their influence, the best.

They are those noble ones who lived
　In that enchanted clime,
Where thoughts are wealth, and structures built
　Of words, shaped into rhyme;
And not of rhymes alone, for in
　Their broad domain uprose
Many a temple, with strong walls,
　From ground to spire, of prose.
And in these temples, eager hearts
　Have found their grandest school,
And restless ones learned strength and peace
　Beneath their gentle rule.

So now you understand, my friend,
　The reason I prefer
The pleasures of this room, o'er those
　A ball room could confer.
If I look up, upon the wall
　I meet their watchful looks;
They speak to me with living force
　From out my treasured books.

Welcome, forever! gentle shades,
　Who, from the courts of Fame,
Hover within my lowly room,
　My loyalty to claim.
Whate'er my lot, where'er I dwell,
　O, fix on me this doom—
Though small my cottage, let there be
　Just one such haunted room.

———◆●◆———

MAGGIE, 1868.

FAIR was the Bishop's daughter!
　Her eyes, so calm and clear,
Revealed a modest dignity,
　A spirit all sincere.
Humble, her chosen duty,
　Within a large, low room,
Day after day, she sat before
　The noisy, busy, loom.

Not as a weary toiler,
　Working alone for bread;
She wrought her task with artist's zeal,
　Blending the colored thread.
Back and forth, as she watched it,
　The shuttle quickly flew;
Across the gray, a crimson thread
　Followed beside the blue;

Here and there, like a shadow,
  Blended the gray and black,
And now and then a line of white
  Followed the shuttle's track.
Bright, in the sunny morning,
  The fresh new pattern shone.
But in the fading sunset's light
  Wore velvet's softer tone.

Weaving the plaided fabric
  For mother's and sister's wear,
She sang, contented and thankful too,
  To ease her parents' care.
Not far away, a mother
  Pondered in anxious care
Over the coming holiday,
  And what to get to wear.

Yet for herself she cared not,
  But for her children, two,
Planning about it by the door,
  Just as little ones do.
There, in the sunshine, drying,
  Hung skeins of brightest blue,
And just enough of snowy white
  To check the whole piece through.

Now she had spun and dyed it,
  To make them dresses new;
The weavers all were overtasked—
  What could the mother do?
And, till the sunset faded,
  The mother dwelt in thought
Upon this humble question, with
  So much importance fraught.

Adown the lane came Maggie,
  Her day of work was through,
Sweet Annie ran to meet her, and
  The baby followed too.
The open gate she entered,
  She was a welcome guest,
The mother brought a chair for each—
  "Children, let Maggie rest."

But no, she took the baby,
  Called Annie to her knee
To tell her what a holiday
  May Day was going to be.
Then, turning to the mother,
  Her thoughtful look she met—
"O! tell me, Marian, if you
  Have made their dresses yet?"

"No," and as she turned swiftly,
  The face's pain to hide,
So Maggie turned, and the long skeins,
  With blank amaze espied.
"Marian! not yet woven?
  Why did you so delay?
I'll take it home with me to-night,
  And weave it right away."

"O Maggie, dear! I cannot
  Let you do this for me,
You've worked too hard, you're paler now
  Than I can bear to see."
"Am I, my father's daughter,
  Yet cannot do this much
For my father's little children?
  Then never call me such."

She gave them her love's labor
  In place of gifts and gold ;
Its value, in the mother's heart,
  Appraised an hundredfold.
Smite ! with the law new written ;
  Strike them with ball and blade ;
Ye cannot sever bonds like this,
  God in the soul has laid.

TO MY FATHER.

And thou art gone !   If thou hadst lived
  This book of mine to read,
Hadst thou approving kissed my cheek,
  I had been praised indeed.
Not lavish were thy gracious words,
  But just and gentle too ;
The timid heart might trust thy smile
  And know thy judgment true.

Thou wert the first of all to speak
  Encouragement to me ;
And in my young life, vision of
  Its future work to see.
Never from thee, upon my heart
  Restraint or chill I felt,
Nor as to an o'erpowering will,
  Beside thy knee I knelt.

How often through those weary months
    When blindness veiled my sight,
Grown weary of the tedious day,
    I waited for the night;
And listened through the mingled sounds
    Thy coming step to wait;
And sometimes thou wouldst, for my sake,
    Some volume's tale relate.

That dreary season past, when I
    ·Roamed wood and field once more,
And homeward brought my trailing vines
    And basket running o'er,
Though with fantastic coronet,
    And strings of floral chain
Wreathed around neck, and arms and waist,
    Thou didst reproof refrain.

And oft while thou wert sleeping yet,
    The sweetest buds I sought,
And to thy plate, at breakfast time,
    With my good morning brought.
To me thou wert embodiment
    Of wisdom, worth and grace;
And I was proud anear thy side,
    Whate'er the throng or place.

How happy would this heart have been,
    To lay within thy hand,
This book of mine; thou best of all,
    My work would understand.
And though all friends should speak of it
    Kindly, still I shall miss
Thy touch of hand, thy gentle word,
    And thine approving kiss.

ACKNOWLEDGMENT.

If aught my pen has traced,
  Has touched thine earnest thought,
As worthy of regard, or praise,
  Through good or beauty taught,
Render that praise to Him,
  Who grants to us to share
Such portion of that brighter light,
  As our frail strength can bear.

To Him for gladness known
  In hearing the " still voice,"
That through all fortunes and all scenes
  Made this weak heart rejoice—
For this, and for the hope
  To better learn the gift,
To use in sacred, grander themes,
  My praise and thanks I lift.

www.ingramcontent.com/pod-product-compliance
Lightning Source LLC
Chambersburg PA
CBHW030810020726
47499CB00006B/1847